THE WOMAN AND THE WARRIOR

VANESSA GRAY BARTAL

DRY CREEK PRESS

PROLOGUE

Summer 1966, A Tiny Town in Rural Alabama

From an early age, he had lived most of his life outdoors. Somehow, the trees always seemed safe. When his old man felt good, which wasn't often these days, he took him into the woods and showed him things—how to hunt, how to track, how to be still. The old man liked to say it was his Indian heritage coming through. John had no idea if that was true. One thing he knew about the old man—he lied, a lot.

His mother never embraced the outdoors, but still somehow he equated her with the woods, too. She was a natural sort of person, her hair long and loose, not done up like the other ladies in town. Transported to another locale, she might be called a hippie. She wasn't, however; she was merely poor. She never wore makeup or fancy clothes, but there was no money for things like that. There was no money for anything. Next year John was thirteen. When he was fourteen, he could get a job, a real one that paid well. For as long as he could remember, it had been his plan to assume the mantle of responsibility, to become the man of the house, picking up the slack for his father who was, more often than not, unavailable these days. If John were being honest, it was better when he wasn't there. Less tension; less terror.

He was away now on a job, or so he said. The days without him were idyllic, but he was always in the back of their minds. After a couple of days, John and his mother would start to look out the window, toward the road, both wondering if he'd be home soon. And more importantly, wondering which version of him they'd receive. Sometimes he brought gifts, things he picked up on the road—a bag of chips from Idaho, a can of peaches from Georgia. Once when John was little, he'd brought a puppy from California. John stared at the wall, blinking. He didn't like to think about that dog, about how it met its end.

But then there were times, more times lately, when he came home angry, sullen, accusing John and his mother of all manner of sins. John's sins were minor—the lawn not mowed properly, the leaves not raked. His mother's sins—John looked at the wall, trying not to think again. His father accused his mother of terrible things, things John knew were untrue. But it didn't matter. In those moments nothing mattered but his anger.

They made it through another evening without his father showing up. After supper, he and his mother played cards. She put on a good show of having fun, but more and more her glance turned toward the window, her laughter growing dimmer, smile pulling tighter.

"You could leave him, you know," John whispered softly.

His mother's face turned sharply to his, brows slamming down. She gave her head a hard shake.

Emboldened, in a rush to get it all out, he continued. "He shouldn't hurt you like he does. It's not right. He could get arrested. We could… we could run away." He half stood, intending to head toward his room and pack a bag.

His mother grabbed his forearm and pulled him back. "Don't. Don't say such things."

He swallowed hard and yanked his arm free. "Why? Why can't we go?"

"Because…" her voice broke and she let out a puff of air. "Because I love him."

He stared at her, one of her eyes droopy from a previous beating, nose permanently crooked, hand clutched to her ribs, sore from the beating he gave before he went away. John felt something within him wither and twist, an anger at her he didn't realize he felt until that moment. "If you won't go, I guess you deserve it."

Her eyes turned stricken, wounded, but he didn't know how to take the harsh words back. And, if he were being honest, it felt good to say them out loud. How could she be so weak? He would never be that weak, never give in to such a useless emotion as love. Confused, frustrated, empty, he turned and went into his room, crawling between the sheets to try and find solace in sleep.

He had no idea what time it was when he was roughly shaken awake, but outside it was dark.

"Run."

His mother pulled the blankets off him and yanked hard on his arm.

"What?" he sat up with a gasp.

"Run." Her voice trembled. She darted a look over her shoulder. "Run into the woods and don't come back until I come find you."

"Mama?" he whispered, voice small and afraid, but she was already moving away from him, pulling up his window. She took his arm and dragged him toward it with more strength than he realized she possessed. "No," he began trying to fight her. "I won't go without you. I'll protect you."

She faced him then, face deathly pale, features set. "You can't. I love you, Johnny. You make me proud in all the ways. Be a good boy and obey. Run, and don't come back." She gave him a shove toward the open window, practically pushing him through.

John didn't want to go, but some instinct propelled him through. And then he heard him, his father's voice, full of rage. Louder, more powerful than it had ever been before, as if he had brought back supernatural powers of wrath from his journey. For a stunned second John and his mother faced each other, eyes locked. *Go,* she mouthed, then put down the window and turned back inside the house.

Sounds came from within, yells, screams, breaking things. Fear took over, and John ran far and fast, his bare feet flying over branches and pinecones. Eventually he paused and bent over, gasping for breath. *What now?* His panicked brain failed to provide an answer. Should he stay? Go back and try to help? Usually he prided himself on being grownup, on handling every situation so he could function as the de facto man of the family. But right now he felt exactly as he was, a twelve-year-old little boy.

Before he could come to a decision, he heard the rush of feet heading in his direction. Once again instinct took over. If his father found him here, out of bed in the middle of the forest, there was no telling what he might do. Quickly, he scrambled up a tree and crouched into a ball, controlling his breathing, becoming as silent as the night.

Except the night wasn't silent, and it wasn't his father who'd pursued him into the woods; it was his mother. She burst into the forest as he had done a few minutes ago, pausing in panicked confusion. Sure she must be looking for him, he unfurled to begin his descent when his father appeared.

His father had always had the almost mythic ability to move in silence, to grow bigger and stronger when angry. He did so now. One moment he and his mother were alone in the woods. The next his father appeared as if from mist, his hand grabbing a fistful of his mother's hair and giving it a hard wrench. She cried out and fell to her knees, begging, pleading for release, for mercy, for anything.

His father's hand cracked hard across her face. The sound of splintering bone reverberated through the woods and, before he could realize what he was doing, John began scrambling down from the tree.

He couldn't see what happened as he climbed down, scraping all the exposed parts of his skin on the tree's rough bark, but his mother had stopped crying. Her noises were worse, more primal. John had been hunting enough times to know a wounded animal when he heard one.

By the time he reached his parents, it was over. His father sat atop his mother, hands around her slack throat, panting, face purple and drenched as his rage finally began to wane. John must have made a sound of his own—a whimper, a mew—because his father whipped in his direction, gun raised, and pointed at the middle of John's body.

For an endless moment they regarded each other in silence. John could read the weight of indecision in his father's face. *Should I kill my son?* It seemed as if he would and then, at the last second, he turned the gun on himself.

"No," John yelled, hand outstretched as he took a step forward. But too late. The shot went off and his father slumped, his lifeless form covering the one beneath him.

John sank to his knees in the moist dirt, staring, mouth agape. Later he wouldn't be able to remember what he felt or thought in those moments or hours after he watched his parents die. And he had no idea why it never occurred to him to leave. Somehow he felt like this was his final duty to them, to stay and keep watch over their bodies. He did it for two days, taking his father's gun and scaring off all manner of animals that tried to approach. Eventually his body began to fade, and he was glad. How could he live with no parents? He didn't want to find out. He curled into a little ball, eyes still on his parents, and that was how the officer found him so many hours later, huddled in a mass, unconscious, gun clutched in his fingers.

They took him to the hospital, cleaned him, fed him, interviewed him, and took him to the place he knew he'd end up, the only foster home he knew in town—the Dunbar family. They were like something from a storybook, a family of eccentrics who were set apart by a number of factors, weird even for a small southern town that elevated weird into an art form. They had a passel of children, but no one knew them because they were all homeschooled, a thing unheard of in those days. As if they didn't have enough kids of their own, they took in troubled kids, too. And now apparently orphans.

John arrived on their doorstep stony and mute, but they welcomed him warmly, bringing him in as they introduced him to their many kids. He would never remember their names, didn't care to try. What was the point? They were nothing to him.

A baby toddled forward and wrapped herself around his leg. John stared down at her, debating the merits of kicking her away. Her golden blond ringlets were a mass of tangles and she smelled like maple syrup. Grimacing, he looked around for a rescue. Surely someone would see how uncomfortable he was. Someone would peel the kid off his leg.

But they didn't. The father of the family beamed his approval. "Looks like Juniper's taken a shine to you."

Juniper. He might have known the weird family would give their kid a weird name. The little girl in question pried her face off his calf and tipped it to inspect him. "Bear," she declared, and then she opened her mouth and bit him.

CHAPTER 1

S ummer 1986, A Tiny Town in Rural Honduras

"*S*ir, the men are dropping like flies."

Major John Caruthers stared at the man, trying to hold his temper. He took a breath and then another. The man started to squirm and it was all John could do not to reach out and smack him. Weakness in any form made him see red. They were soldiers. Why was he the only one who seemed to comprehend that? "Why?"

"Sir?"

"I said why. Why are my soldiers, if such could be called that, dropping like flies, Sergeant?"

Now the man really started to squirm. "It's a hundred and ten degrees, sir. The humidity alone…And provisions, are, well, sir…"

"I understand," John said, nodding, and the sergeant sighed with relief that was short lived when John continued. "I mean, after all, we are here on vacation, aren't we, Sergeant?"

"Uh…" the sergeant began, confused by John's congenial tone.

"And there certainly aren't any natives nearby who live and work in these conditions all the time, who are likely laughing at these so called trained men complaining about a little heat."

"Well, see, uh…"

"Would you like me to turn up the air conditioning? Maybe order some ice cream?"

"Uh…" the man looked around the canvas tent, its flaps not fluttering in the thick, lifeless air.

The major placed his palms on the rickety desk and leaned forward. His voice dropped to a silky whisper. "Or would it be possible for the men to remember they are the most highly trained soldiers from the greatest country on earth, sent here on a mission of dire importance? Would you like me to come out there and tell them in person how I feel about grumbling and complaints, Sergeant?"

"Er, no, sir, I think I begin to understand." With effort, he resisted the urge to tug his collar.

"Very well then, Sergeant, you are dismissed." They shared the requisite salute and the sergeant back stepped out of the tent, resisting the urge to genuflect and tremble. He darted out of the tent and bent over, attempting to suck oxygen that wasn't there. *There is no air in this country*, he thought, then immediately banished it lest The Major somehow gain the ability to see into his mind and hear the complaint.

"Did you tell him?" His buddy, Ackers, slipped up on his side and bent over to whisper in his ear. So far no one had been able to prove The Major heard everything that went on in the camp, but it seemed so. The men had taken to whispering everything like middle school girls at a sleepover.

The sergeant shook his head.

"You've got to," Ackers said, giving him a nudge.

"He'll kill me," the sergeant said. "You don't know. You just don't know."

"It's going to be worse if you don't tell him now," Ackers hissed.

The sergeant pressed his lips together and shook his head. The stories about Major John Caruthers had circulated for years, becoming myth and legend—how he could go so stealth you never sensed him coming, how he tended to make troublesome people disappear forever, how he seemingly never ate, slept, or drank. The man was cast iron; he had no weaknesses, no family, never took time off, never took a break, had been involved in every major military operation since Vietnam, and had somehow turned every one in his favor. Had so many confirmed kills people stopped keeping count. Before this assignment, he'd been excited to work with the man. *Excited.* And now...now he wanted to get home in one piece. It said something that he feared his commanding officer much more than he feared the rebels and insurgents all around them.

Ackers squared his shoulders and stared toward the tent flap, the light of challenge in his eyes. "Fine, I'll tell him."

"Godspeed," the sergeant said, still trying to draw a deep breath. Ackers took a step into the tent. The sergeant began a mental countdown. By the time he reached a hundred, Ackers had been tossed back through the flap, landing hard in the dirt at the sergeant's feet. "How'd he take it?" he couldn't help but ask.

Ackers didn't answer. He clutched his stomach and retched, turning his head in time to heave into the grass.

⚷

he girl won't go.

That was the information the man imparted before John tossed him from the tent. He might not have tossed him, if he hadn't been the last one sent to retrieve her. But he had personally failed and therefore had received his just due. John couldn't tolerate failure any more than he could tolerate weakness. When he assigned a task, he expected it to be carried out, no excuses, no mistakes. They were the armed forces of the United States of America. The world expected nothing less than perfection from them, and Major John Caruthers would provide it or die trying. He didn't care how many people he had to take with him along the way.

For a moment, he pondered leaving the woman behind. She was one lone botanist. How bad would it be, really, if they left her behind? But then his conscience smote him. *She's an American.* That fact alone meant John and his men were honor bound to protect her, whether she wanted their protection or not.

The problem was, he'd sent four men. Four men had tried and failed to evacuate the little chit, and she'd somehow charmed them all into going away again without her.

"She says she wants to stay," the idiot before this one informed him.

"It's not her choice to make," John had roared. Morons, all around. Some days he felt like he was drowning in them. They had a job to do, a clear cut job. What was so hard about following through and doing it? *People mess everything up,* he thought. It wasn't the first time he'd thought such and it wouldn't be the last because people always tended toward stupidity. No matter the country, no matter the language, no matter the demographic, people would always be as stupid and helpless as possible.

I'm going to have to do it myself, he thought, fighting the ever-present rage monster inside him. This girl apparently thought she was something special, able to charm whichever man got in her way. He almost smiled as he imagined all the ways her little plan was about to go awry. *Prepare yourself, lady. You've never met the likes of John Caruthers.*

If he'd known what waited for him, he would have aimed the warning at himself.

Her tent was in the middle of nowhere, begging to be invaded. It was a wonder she hadn't been kidnapped and raped already. If not yet, then soon. John remained hidden a minute, eyeing the tent in annoyance. He was the head of this mission and had a million and one things to do. It irked him greatly to have to tear himself away long enough to pack up some boneheaded scientist.

He stalked to her tent and entered uninvited. In his experience, the element of surprise always gave him the advantage.

Something familiar tickled his nose and he stopped short in the entry of the tent. *Home,* he thought, then quickly shook his head. He had no home. That was what made him a good soldier, his complete lack of attachment.

The woman had her back to him, likely had no idea he was there. It was kind of his thing, to be silent. His calling card, if such could be said about him. He cleared his throat, but when she turned, there was no surprise in her expression, only amusement. They studied each other a few blinks, assessing. She was short and petite, except her hair, blond and curly and spilling out of its confinement. She wore glasses, and he wondered anew at the desperation of his men because, though cute, she wasn't a knockout by any means. Pretty, but not a pinup.

More scientist than siren. He opened his mouth to tell her once and for all it was time to go, but she preempted him.

"John Caruthers, as I live and breathe."

He blinked at her, as much surprise as he ever showed anyone. Had his men blabbed? How else to explain her recognition of him? "Ma'am," he said. Was his voice always so stern and gravely, or was it only in comparison to hers, the first female he'd talked to in months.

She smiled, one of her cheeks revealing a deep dimple. "You don't recognize me."

"Ma'am," he said, different intonation this time, a question.

"This is too good. I wonder how long I can keep you in suspense."

"I assure you, ma'am, I feel no such emotion," he said.

She snickered, nose wrinkling. "Look at you, all militarized. And calling me ma'am. This is a twist."

Her accent was familiar, and he felt a prickle of foreboding. America was a vast nation. It was not possible he wound up in the jungle with someone from so near his home. And yet she knew him. At last his curiosity was piqued, but his mind drew a blank. She looked like no one he knew, and he had an excellent memory.

"Ma'am," he repeated, and this time the tone bordered on exasperation.

"Haven't figured it out yet, huh?" she said, smug.

Only years of practice and training kept his ascetic countenance in place. It wasn't so much that he couldn't place her as her enjoyment at his expense. John prided himself on being the smartest person in the room, always.

"Would you like me to give you a hint?"

His expression didn't flicker.

Her smile widened. She placed her hands on her hips and leaned forward, tilting on the balls of her feet to whisper, "Bear."

He blinked at her once, twice, three times. "Juniper Dunbar?"

"One and the same," she said, smile growing impossibly wider.

"Last time I saw you, you were…" he trailed off, uncharacteristically uncertain.

"Eight."

"And now you're…"

"Twenty two. And you are…"

"Thirty two."

"Old," she declared, and his brows lowered. Thirty two was not old by anyone's estimation, except possibly someone who was only twenty two. "Why'd you go away and never come back? You promised you would always come back."

He heard it then, the same imperious, wheedling tone she'd used when she was eight. *Why are you going away, Bear? Don't you love us?* "I've been a mite busy, Juniper. The world doesn't save itself."

"Oh, my lands."

That was all she said, forcing him to draw her out. "What?"

"You've become pompous."

"I've become factual."

"You were always that. Now it's somethin' else, somethin' unpleasant. It's going to take a lot of work on my part to deconstruct you, Bear."

"No, because, see," he held out his arm for her inspection. "This uniform means I'm here to work, which brings me to my purpose for this visit. You have to go."

She tipped her head at him, smiling sweetly. "No."

"It's amazing you were able to find the question in that directive. Let me try again." He took a step closer and stared down at her, channeling his old drill instructor. "You have to go."

She took a step closer and stood on her toes, widening her smile. "No."

"Are you unaware of what's happening in Honduras in this year of our Lord, 1986?"

"So many fascinating things," she said, shifting back onto her heels.

"It's practically in all-out war with Nicaragua. The president has ordered this area evacuated. That means you, Juniper."

"I'm not leaving my work. I'm certain it will all blow over."

"I don't think you understand what my presence here means," he said.

"I do, actually. It's fate."

"No, I...what?"

"How else do you explain two long-lost acquaintances from middle-of-nowhere Alabama meeting up in the jungles of Honduras?"

"I've been in Central America practically the past ten years, when I wasn't in Africa."

She gasped. "Which part? I love Africa. Oh, John, you have to tell me all about it."

"No, I don't, and no, I won't because, see, I go places in secret. That's what I do, that's why I'm *here*." He pointed to the ground between them.

"If it's a secret, why are you telling me?" she asked.

"Because I had to come see for myself in person who was so ridiculous four of my men failed to uproot her," he ground out.

"And it's me. Surprise!" She waved her hands in the air, beaming at him.

"No, that's not...I came here because...You can't..." He couldn't remember the last time anyone in his life made him stammer. Sucking a breath, he found his center and tried again. "You have a generous ten minutes to pack what you deem essential, and then we're leaving."

"You're cute, Bear. But no," she replied unconcernedly, turning her back on him, a mistake. She reached for a mug, but he grabbed her arm, halting her. "My, but you're silent," she said. Her glance fell on his fingers, now wrapped around her forearm. Impossibly, almost against his will, he saw himself release her, one finger at a time. "Would you like some coffee? I picked and dried it myself."

"No," he ground out.

"I think you should. If there's one thing I remember about you, it's how grumpy you get when you're hungry. My lands, I've never seen the like of you first thing in the morning, John, hungry and uncaffeinated."

"You can't possibly remember," he rasped. It had been so long since anyone mentioned that time in his life, his beginnings. He had taken great pains to erase his past, and now here it was, standing before him with a beaming smile.

"You'd be surprised what I remember," she said.

He stared at her, momentarily dumbfounded while she poured a cup of coffee and set a piece of bread on a plate. And then she handed it to him like they were taking tea together.

"It's banana bread," she said when he failed to reach for the plate. "The locals think I'm some kind of magician because I bake it in my outdoor oven. I've promised to teach them my ways in exchange for access to their knowledge." She broke off a little piece of the bread and shoved it between her lips.

Absently, he reached for the plate and started to eat. He hadn't had banana bread since he went to West Point, hadn't had sugar, really. Sweets made a person soft, and John Caruthers was anything but soft. But now, standing in her hut eating a fresh, fat slice of bread, he wondered why he'd been holding out. Had anything ever tasted so good? He honestly couldn't remember.

"What kind of knowledge?" he asked. As far as he could tell, all the locals knew was how to keep their heads down and avoid gunfire, something Juniper could probably do well to learn.

"Plants, trees, medicine, herbs. Anything and everything they have to bestow. I want to know it all."

He glanced down at the delicate plate in his oversized hands, chagrined to realize he'd eaten the entire slice of bread. Without asking, Juniper sliced another piece and slid it onto his plate. "I don't eat sweets," he murmured, reaching for the second slice. When he finished that slice, she took the plate and filled his hands instead with warm coffee the color of a coconut.

"What did you put in it?" he asked, grimacing.

"Goat milk and date sugar."

"Disgusting," he said, but he tipped it back and drained it. And then he stood there blinking, momentarily forgetting his mission, a thing which had never happened to him in all his years of military life.

"I used to believe I would marry you," Juniper said softly.

His brows rose. "Why would you think that?"

"Because I thought you belonged to me and, maybe, that I belonged to you, too."

"Surely by now you've realized that was incorrect. I belong to no one. And you…" Suddenly he remembered why he was there and snapped to attention with a scowl. "You have to go. What on earth are you doing here in the first place?"

"The kapoks," she said.

"What?"

She pointed behind her. "The kapok trees. They're invaluable. I've been sent here to research them as part of my graduate fellowship."

"What?"

"Thirty two seems young to lose your hearing," she said.

"I heard you, I simply don't believe you. You're risking your life, defying orders, for some overgrown trees?"

"Am I risking my life because there's danger or merely by virtue of defying your orders?" she asked.

"At this point it's a tossup," he said.

She burst into giggles.

"I'm not joking," he said.

"That's what makes it funny," she said, dabbing beneath her eyes. "Oh, John, it's really hard to take you seriously when I used to ride on your back when we swam."

"I don't understand what that has to do with this present moment," he said.

"Are you…" she leaned closer, tipping her head, "Are you blushing?"

"Absolutely no," he said.

"You're adorable."

Never, in his entire life, had anyone called him adorable. He glanced down, the blasted delicate cup still cradled in his too big fingers. *What am I doing?* For the first time in his life, he felt like he might be having an out of body experience. He set the plate on the counter and backstepped out of the tent, his eyes remaining solidly on Juniper Dunbar.

CHAPTER 3

"Is she gone, sir?" his sergeant greeted him when he returned to camp.

"She's...preparing her things." He brushed by the sergeant and strode into his tent, sinking wearily into his chair. John hated liars, and now he had become one. Because of Juniper Dunbar.

He wanted to be angry, to rail at all the trouble she was causing him, but he couldn't. The shock was too great. Juniper Dunbar, here, in the middle of Honduras. What were the chances?

"There must be some logical explanation." He said the words out loud. They made him feel better. Unconsciously, he patted the book in his pocket, the one he always kept on him. It was the foundation on which he'd built his life: logic, sweet, unadulterated logic. It never failed him, never led him astray. Unlike those pesky emotions and *fate*, as Juniper had termed it. Yuck, no thank you. John was nobody's fool. He knew better than to build his life on such insubstantial nonsense. People who did that were no better than... He pushed the thought away, refusing to remember his mother.

He would have to go back, to tell her once again and in no uncertain terms that she had to go. It was a directive, straight from the top. All civilians had to evacuate the area. The decree made no exceptions for cute scientists. John made no exception to the rules, ever. Rules were life; they kept the world sane, his world especially. He was certain that if he once again explained the situation to Juniper and told her to go, he would succeed. After all, she was now part of his mission, and John had never failed at a mission before. The ripe age of thirty two was no time to begin. *And thirty two is not old,* he silently assured himself. He was in better shape than most of the boys who came from basic, could outrun, outmaneuver, outlast any of them. And he had, many times. Until someone better came along and knocked him off his throne, Major John Caruthers was in charge, in all the ways. The sooner Juniper Dunbar learned that, the better. Now, away from her influence, he could see all the ways she'd befuddled him. The coffee, the food, the blinding turns in conversation. Tomorrow he'd be the one in charge like usual, he was certain.

Thus decided, he reached for a map and returned his attention once again to work. The army always made sense; studying tactic brought him a dose of much needed security. *She's only one girl. How much more trouble could she cause?*

His mind began to unsettle again. He forced it to the map and to sweet, blessed work.

"*J*ohn, how delightful to see you."

He stopped short in the entry of her tent, momentarily thrown off kilter. People were never delighted to see him. They were shocked, terrified, and universally filled with dread. His eyes narrowed suspiciously on her, bedecked today in some native-looking dress, her hair already tumbling free of its confinement. Her nose wrinkled, but not in distaste. Instead it was some practiced move to push up her glasses without using her hands. "Juniper," he began, tone stern, but she interrupted him.

"I feel I owe you an apology," she said, all humble meekness.

"You…you do?"

She nodded. "Our first meeting in fourteen years, and I didn't even hug you." She propelled herself at him and he caught her by instinct because that was what you did when threatening objects hurled toward your body. You put your hands up, trying to deflect. There was no deflecting Juniper, however. She tossed herself at him, wrapping her arms tightly around his neck, dangling. He was taller, so she hung off him like a human clothes hanger. He attempted to set her away; she refused to be put down. He sat, hoping that would break her hold. It didn't. Her body folded into his, sliding comfortably onto his lap like the toddler she'd once been. Her head rested on his shoulder.

"You're not hugging me in return," she noted.

"No," he agreed.

She pulled away, tipping her face as she made her inspection. "Don't tell me you've forgotten how. I'm certain my family tried to teach you."

That was undoubtedly true. The Dunbars were huggers, all of them. They had lavished hugs on him every day of the six years he'd lived in their house, never caring they weren't returned. John had stood stock still, arms at his sides, tolerating the affection in discomfort. Except with Juniper, of course. It would have been odd not to hug a baby, and she'd been a baby then. Now, however…

It was still odd not to reciprocate. So, despite his best efforts not to, he found his arms curving around her, drawing her slightly closer. Sighing happily now, she settled back against him, resting her head on his shoulder.

"Juniper," he began, aiming for sternness again. If he'd succeeded in finding it, it would have been a feat, indeed, cuddled together as they now were. But before he could try, she preempted him again.

"Also, I forgot to thank you."

"Thank…me?" It was as if he'd forgotten how to speak to humans and had to learn all over again, he realized, which was partly true. There weren't a lot of women in his world, and the ones who were found him too terrifying to do more than drop their eyes and scurry away. Those were the smart ones, he thought. Not like Juniper who seemed to be lacking self-preservation completely.

She pulled away, beaming as she regarded him. "It's because of you

I became a botanist."

"Me?" he repeated.

She nodded. "All those walks we took in the woods, remember? You taught me so many things, about how to listen, how to appreciate, how to be still."

"That one apparently didn't take," he noted dryly. Juniper was the same live wire she had always been, an unstoppable force of energy, movement in every molecule of her being, sharp contrast to John's unending stillness. The youngest child in a family of animated extroverts, she had almost been too much for even them to handle. They had seemed all too happy to foist her on John, not that Juniper had given anyone any choice in the matter. She had attached herself to him that first day and never let go, practically becoming his shadow the remaining six years he lived with her family. Where John went, Juniper was there. When it became clear she couldn't keep up, he carried her. They had been inseparable, and yet he had left when he was eighteen and never looked back, secure in the knowledge that Juniper was too little to have any lasting memory of him, secure in the fact she wouldn't miss him. But if the way she now clung to him like a koala was any indication, perhaps she had. For the first time in a long time, maybe decades, he began to feel something he thought he would never feel again—empathy. It must have hurt her when he went away and didn't return. For that he was sorry, but he didn't want to be sorry; he didn't want to be anything. He had spent every day since he was twelve trying to cut emotion from his life with surgical precision. And he had succeeded admirably. Absolutely no one who met him would ever accuse him of being sentimental, of being a softy. Yet here he sat in a tent in the middle of the jungle, a stubborn little botanist planted firmly in his grasp.

He stood so abruptly Juniper tumbled to the ground in an untidy heap. "You have to go," he declared.

"But it's my tent," she said, blinking up at him in amused dismay.

"No, you know what I mean. You have to leave, to evacuate. Now. Today."

"That's really not possible," she said, and then she smiled. For a moment, he got caught up staring at her dimple. He had seen that dimple more times than he could count, had never paid special attention to it before. But now… He felt the sudden and unbidden need to touch his finger to it, to measure its depth against his knuckle. His fingers flexed, itching. He curled them into fists and took a step away. He raised his finger, pointing it accusingly at her.

"Last warning, Juniper. You have to go."

"I don't think so, Bear."

There were times, like now, when he became so angry he saw everything through a hazy red filter. Usually it worked like some sort of danger signal to the person in his path, a warning to back off. Juniper, of course, had never properly understood nor heeded danger. It had complicated John's life as a child, trying hard to keep her alive when she seemed bent on destruction. At age four she did a cannonball into a gator-infested river, forcing him to dive in after her. Never in his wildest imagination did he dream he would continue his crusade as an adult.

"Juniper, you can't imagine what you're doing." His tone had turned soft and silky. To anyone who knew him, it was a red flag. The quieter he became, the deadlier he was about to be.

"You look exactly the same," Juniper said, eyes big behind her glasses as she studied him. "I thought I imagined you bigger, stronger, more powerful, but no. If anything, I underestimated. A soldier. I'm so proud of you."

He blinked, the red haze fading to a rosy shade of pink. "Thank you. I mean, no. I mean, stop changing the subject."

"I wasn't trying to. It's just that we have so much to catch up on. Fourteen years is a long time to be away from home, John."

He pressed his thumb into his thigh, trying to focus all his aggravation on that spot instead of the girl in front of him. "That's not my home, Juniper. This is my home." Belatedly he realized he made the motion around her tent. Juniper grinned up at him, delighted.

"Of course it is. Wherever I am is home to you, always. And vice versa."

He shook his head like he was trying to clear his inner ear after a dive gone wrong. "No, that's not...The army is my home. Not Alabama. Not with you."

"Your accent is making a return," she uttered in a conspiratorial whisper.

"No, it's not," he drawled and pressed his lips together to hide his annoyance. He had taken great pains to lose his accent at West Point. Southerners were seen as kindly, warm, gentle. John hadn't wanted any part of those descriptors. Accurate, precise, deadly. That was what he was, a robot without a past, without a history. Except now his history had caught up and now laughed up at him from her perch on the floor.

"You're so handsome," she added cheerfully.

"And you are..." he pointed a finger, ready to blast her, but he couldn't figure out how best to do it. Juniper had always been impossible to repel. It was how they'd ended up spending so much time together when he was a kid. He would push her away and she would bounce right back, again and again until she eventually wore him down and he gave up. In all his life she was the only person who had ever beaten his will, had worn him to a nub so acquiescence became the easier and more preferred route. And she was doing it again now. "You're a child," he declared.

She sprang up and dusted her behind. "I'm a college graduate."

"You're twenty two. I have socks older than that."

She wrinkled her nose. "The army should really think about paying you better if you've felt the need to hold on to socks for two decades."

"That's not...I don't...Juniper!"

"What?" She blinked up at him with feigned innocence. They were toe to toe now and he felt...he wasn't certain what he felt, nor why he felt so much to begin with. His heart was usually closed off, inaccessible to everyone, himself included. He didn't like that Juniper had so easily wormed her way in, if only to make him feel annoyed. Major John Caruthers didn't get annoyed, and certainly not with a tiny slip of a girl, a scientist, no less. He pressed his hand to his chest and took a breath. His hand rested reassuringly on his book, like a touchstone.

Outside problems were merely that, outside. They could only trouble him as much as he let them. Therefore, he wouldn't let them.

"Juniper."

"Bear."

"I know you think you have some kind of misplaced crush on me," he began reasonably, but was once again interrupted by her.

"No, I don't."

He blinked at her. "What?"

"Not that you bothered to ask after my wellbeing, but I'm engaged."

"To a man?"

"I tried getting engaged to a lizard, but it was highly frowned upon," she said.

"Then why are you here?"

"Because I'm working. Surely you of all people can understand the importance of work." She tipped her head. "Don't tell me you won't let your wife work."

"You know I'm not married," he said.

"But when you get married, you plan to keep her under lock and key."

"I plan to never get married."

"Why?" she said, sounding wounded.

"Lots of reasons. The important thing is…" What was the important thing? He couldn't remember. What had they been discussing? "When is the wedding?"

"When I get back," she said, turning to the side. When she faced him again, it was to stuff something between his lips, some kind of sweet bread that tasted like coconut. He chewed thoughtfully, swallowing as if by rote.

"What kind of man is he?"

"A biochemist."

"That tells me what he does, not what sort of man he is."

"What would tell you that?" she asked.

"Would he give his life for you?"

She blinked at him. "I suppose I never thought about it."

"Juniper, think about it." He tried to say it sternly, but she stuffed another bite of cake in his mouth. It was hard to be stern and eat cake.

"I'm pretty good at taking care of myself, Bear. Not often in need of rescue."

"Don't be one of those women," he said.

"I thought you said I was a girl," she reminded him.

"Don't be one of those girls."

"What girls?" she asked.

"The kind who is so independent you won't listen to reason or be taken care of," he said.

"I suppose I'd like to believe relationships are a mutual taking care of each other. Hasn't that been your experience?"

He didn't tell her it hadn't been his experience because he had never been in a relationship, would never be in a relationship. She stuffed another bite of cake into his mouth. He waited to chew and swallow to speak. "How would he feel knowing you're standing in a tent in Honduras, feeding cake to me?"

"He'd be delighted," she said.

"He would?"

She nodded. "I told him all about you, of course. He'd be thrilled I finally found you."

"Somehow I doubt it," he said.

"Why?"

"Because I'm the kind of guy they send in when they need to make certain a job gets done. People like me, we're not well liked. We don't have friends."

"I like you. We're friends." She fed him the last of the cake and looked about for a place to wipe her fingers. In every memory he had of her, she was always sticky with something—syrup, jam, candy. He had spent half his life wiping her face and hands and now was no exception. He reached for the basin of water, wet a cloth, and wiped her fingers. "Thank you."

"I could see you gearing up to wipe your hand on my shirt," he said.

"She bit her lip, repressing her grin. "You're so ever-loving tidy,

Bear. It makes me want to tousle you."

She was perpetually tousled, then, still, and she never seemed to mind. As he stared at her, one of her curls popped free of its clasp and landed on her eyelid. Juniper appeared not to notice. John let go of one of her hands and pushed the curl, holding the hair aloft off her face. "How can you stand that?"

They were still toe to toe, her hand in his, his free hand pushing the hair out of her eyes. When he finally zeroed in on her expression, it was so intense, so pained he inhaled a sharp breath, bringing the scent of her deep into his lungs. "You used to call me Juni," she whispered.

"That was a long time ago," he whispered, his thumb smoothing along her brow.

"I went to West Point," she declared.

"What?"

"I called them, wrote to them. They wouldn't answer. I thought if I could see them in person they might tell me where you went."

"Most of where I've been is classified," he said. Why were they whispering? He had no idea. "Why were you trying to find me so bad?"

"Because I needed you."

He almost smiled. He somehow should have guessed Juniper would wind up being one of those women given to high romance and drama. The wild exuberance of her childhood had apparently found an outlet in fantasy, one where she set him up as the dashing romantic lead, at least until her chemist came along. "I don't think you demanded the sort of rescue I would have provided," he said.

"It's been fourteen years. You don't know what I needed." This time she was the one to step away, again and again until she bumped the canvas wall of the tent, her eyes remaining locked on him. "Good-bye, John. Take care."

He needed to tell her to go, to leave, to clear out. But there was something so wounded and vulnerable in her expression, he held his tongue. Next time, he would make her understand. She closed her eyes and inhaled. When she opened them again, he was gone.

CHAPTER 4

He put a pin in the map and had to take it back out again because he had no idea what he'd marked or why.

Blast Juniper Dunbar.

The woman was like a brain worm, constantly wriggling to mind when he tried to think of other things. He was supposed to be plotting rebel target sites on a map. Instead he stared vaguely, pin in hand, poking uselessly in and out of the map. Like a squirmy child who can't sit still and focus. Worse, like an idiot lovestruck soldier.

Not love, annoyance, he assured himself. The woman worked his ever loving last nerve and it was so aggravating that she got to him that it got to him even more, doubling down on the annoyance.

"Sir."

The sergeant's interruption startled John, causing his hand to slip and jab his thumb with the pin. He expelled a word and popped his thumb in his mouth, sucking off the drop of blood. When he regarded his sergeant, the man was already in a flop sweat, terrified John would once again dropkick him through the tent flap. In his current mood, it was a worthwhile fear.

"S-sorry," the man stuttered and then, remembering John hated that fear stammer, cleared his throat and took a breath. "Pardon the interruption, sir. Someone here to see you."

John's brain scrambled, trying to think who on earth would visit this remote location. "Brass?" Had the higher ups come with a new directive?

The sergeant cleared his throat again. "It's, uh, Juniper, sir."

John's eyes narrowed on him, not enjoying the familiarity of her name on his lips. "Please show Miss Dunbar in."

"Yes, sir," the man replied, genuflecting his way backwards through the flap.

A moment later he reappeared with Juniper, who looked and smelled fresh and pretty, despite the oppressive heat. John caught a whiff of something clean, tropical, and sweet. Did she bathe in the river like the locals? That was definitely unsafe, what with all the crocodiles and enemy combatants wandering around. But he couldn't otherwise account for her fresh and spotless demeanor, unless she'd found some way to magic indoor plumbing the way she'd found a way to bake.

He realized, belatedly, that he had been staring stock still while he made his inspection and had these thoughts, his gaze fastened on Juniper, some might say hungrily. And his sergeant was there, privy to everything. With a nod, he dismissed the man.

"Actually, he can stay, if it's okay," Juniper interrupted, resting her hand gently on the man's forearm. "It concerns him, too."

John focused on that hand on that arm. Why was she touching him? Was she making a play for all the men in the camp? That would explain what had them all so addled in her presence, in addition to the fact that she was the only woman for miles. His eyes narrowed on the sergeant who took a step away from Juniper and gulped so loudly John could hear it from across the room. Where did the army get these gutless boys?

"May I?" Juniper asked, reaching for the chair across from his desk.

John indicated the chair with a flourish and everyone sat, Juniper and the sergeant on one side, him on the other. He had the idea she was waiting for him to speak, so of course he didn't. He folded his hands and waited her out.

She folded her hands, too, no doubt mimicking him, and dimpled a beaming smile. "So, Major Caruthers."

It was somewhat startling to hear her call him that, but he didn't let on. He'd developed a good poker face by the time he entered kindergarten. His father hadn't liked any form of whining or crying. John had learned early to hold it inside and reveal nothing. The army had only enhanced that skill. "Miss Dunbar," he said, tone remote and civil.

She leaned forward and flattened her palm on the table. "My mother was famous for her pecan pie."

That was unexpected, but John didn't show it. He well remembered her mother's pie. Pecan had been his favorite, the treat she made him every year on his birthday.

Juniper tipped her head to study him, more than a hint of amusement in her features. "Have you ever had pecan pie, Major Caruthers?"

"A time or two," John said, certain she remembered it was his favorite. The woman was like an elephant; she seemingly never forgot anything. Beside her his sergeant shifted, as if shocked by the bombshell revelation that his commanding officer enjoyed pie. His men had probably never seen him eat pie, but not because he didn't like it. More because he was picky about it. Army pie could hardly be considered such. He'd rather do without than spoil his memories and taste buds with rotten pie.

"I recently came into possession of a large amount of native cashews," Juniper declared.

"That does not surprise me at all, Miss Dunbar. I definitely think nuts when I think of you," John said.

"Now Major Caruthers," she chastised, knocking the desk between them. "You are going to cause me to renege on my fun surprise."

"I shudder to ask what 'fun surprise' you might be referring to," John said.

"For some reason, I've been thinking a whole lot about home and those pecan pies my mama used to make for special occasions, and there wasn't anything for it until I tried to recreate one, using what I had on hand. I think cashews are a fair substitution, and I came to seek an expert opinion."

"You baked a pie," he said slowly.

She shook her head.

"No?" he pressed. The woman's mind wasn't natural. It was like it worked in riddles and everything had to be unwound.

"I baked four pies," she said. "Tell me, how many men are in this camp?"

The sergeant opened his mouth to answer, but John barked, "That's classified."

"Oh," Juniper said, once again amused. "I can see why. You wouldn't want anyone to bake poison pies, take out the whole platoon. Battalion? Brigade? Unit? Team? Squad?"

"You're quite the walking thesaurus, Miss Dunbar."

"I had a good teacher, Major Caruthers."

"One who was a bit too lax on discipline, in my estimation," he said.

"I had a strict one until I was eight. When he disappeared, I traded up," she said.

He knew she meant her father had taught her fulltime after he graduated and left for the army, and yet the way she said it made him wonder if there had been some other boy or man to take his place. Someone else she spent all her waking hours with. As much as he tried not to let it, the thought left a sour taste in his mouth. Of course he hadn't wanted Juniper to be his constant tagalong and sidekick back then. But neither did he want her to be anyone else's. Juniper had been the family pet; there was something special about being her chosen someone. It had made the rest of the family, and even people in town, look at him like he was something exceptional for being her choice.

"I brought the pies, in case you were wondering," she said when he didn't reply.

"I wasn't, but now I am. How did you get four pies here?"

"I tied them in a bundle and carried them on my back like a little papoose."

"You walked three miles through the jungle with pie on your back?" the sergeant said, sounding a little too awed for John's tastes.

"And where are these alleged pies right now?" John asked. If his mouth now watered, it was because it was lunchtime, not because all he could think of was pie, the sort her mother used to make. If John had one weakness, and to be clear he did not, but if he did, it would be pie. Somehow he thought Juniper knew and was using it against him.

"I left them with the men."

John and his sergeant traded glances. "They'll destroy them," the sergeant said, sounding wounded. The men were like a horde of locusts when it came to food, devouring everything in their path. Those pies wouldn't be safe with them. Fistfights could break out. "Permission to go and check, sir?"

John gave him a nod and watched as the man flew out of his chair so fast it was like watching an ejection seat on a fighter jet.

"Oh, no," Juniper said, hand to her cheek. "They'll probably eat them all. Shoot, it's probably too late and you won't get any. Oh, well. It's not like you're a big fan of sweets or pie in particular. Are you, Bear?" She tipped her head and regarded him, equal parts insolent and adorable.

"You know I am," he ground out. Blast her and her ways, making him yearn for pie and then taking it away.

She gasped and covered her mouth. "Oh, that's right. You were always partial to Mama's pie. I can't say I did hers justice, but hopefully I came close."

"It's rather a moot point now, isn't it, Juniper?" he asked, resisting the urge to kick the desk. *I want pie!* That was now the new number one refrain running through his brain which, despite the letdown of not being able to get any, was still better than the previous refrain of *JuniperJuniperJuniper* that had been playing since he first stepped into her tent.

"You look a little miffed, Major. Are you miffed? I mean, surely a high and mighty officer such as yourself doesn't get put out over a little thing like pie. Does he?"

"Woman, you are poking at a thing you'd best leave alone, if you know what's good for you," John warned.

She laughed, a Juniper burble of delight that at some other time might have made him smile. Now, hungry and cranky as he was, it made him see red. "You're assuming I have any idea what's good for me."

Before he could respond to that, she reached into a bag at her feet, deposited an entire pie on the desk before him, and leaned forward to whisper in his ear. "A good southern girl always bakes a secret fifth pie for the people who are most special." She straightened and tossed him a little wink and a little wave. "Goodbye, Major Caruthers. I do hope it will be an extra good day."

John didn't say a word as she exited his tent. He sat still for exactly thirty seconds, until he was certain she was well and truly away, then reached into his drawer, pulled out a fork, and ate his pie straight from the tin.

CHAPTER 5

The Major had no need to go to the market, at least not for himself. He had zero needs for which the army didn't provide, from shaving cream to clothing, it was all covered. But he went to the market regardless, walking the open air stalls each week as a sign of goodwill to the locals. He bought things he never used, for that same sense of community. Most of the women who sold their wares had no other source of income. His need to provide for them trumped his desire not to buy things he didn't need. *"Bonita, bonita,"* he said, nodding as a woman stuffed a woven purse into his fingers, beaming. He gave her more than it was worth, not enough to be insulting or obvious, but enough to make himself seem ignorant of how much things cost. She beamed at him, a little stunned, and he turned away, not wanting to see gratitude for something so simple.

It was in that turn that he saw her, a flash of blond curls. He didn't believe in auras, but if he did Juniper's would be sparkling. She radiated energy, movement, and good cheer. John was so focused on staring at her it took a moment to realize to whom she talked. And when he did his heart somersaulted for other, more sinister reasons. *Slovenka.* It wasn't his real name. Or maybe it was, John had no idea. The Eastern Bloc had become masters at misinformation. Whatever his name, he was John's Soviet counterpart, the man sent from the USSR to oversee the Sandinistas, the man now fueling all the unrest John attempted to keep a lid on. They were polar opposites, enemies of the highest order. Of *course* he would find Juniper. This was what John feared, that someone would figure out their connection and use it against him.

Though, as he studied the two as they talked, neither seemed aware of him. They chatted like old friends, both faces alight with animation. He said something that made her laugh, and she said something that made him chuckle in return. John clenched his fists, fighting a losing battle with some darker emotion. *Not jealousy*, he assured himself. Juniper was free to talk to whomever she chose. It was merely that she chose to talk to this man, his enemy.

He realized, belatedly, that he needed to turn away and disappear before they saw him. Because if Slovenka saw the way he now stared at Juniper—like a lovesick idiot—he would know, he would understand she was somehow meaningful to John.

He pivoted and strode away, but too late. Three long strides later, he heard his name on her lips. And his idiot heart flipped with the knowledge that she had walked away from Slovenka to call after him. He was all set to ignore her, a thing which would doubtless enrage her. Confirmation of that rage arrived in the form of a piece of rotten fruit to the back of his head. He stopped short and pivoted again, this time facing Juniper.

She stood in the middle of the aisle of the market. Everyone had apparently witnessed her assault on him because everyone now stood aside, ogling them, even as they gave them a wide berth. They squared off like two actors in a western movie, about to have a duel. And that was how John felt, as if the showdown that had been hovering between them was now about to begin. Juniper realized it too, with more than a hint of panic. He wondered if she regretted her rash act because, as soon as he faced her and planted his hands on his hips, she immediately dropped her offending arm, the one that had hurled the fruit, and tucked it behind her back, pressing her lips together.

"Well, hey, fancy seeing you here," she said, aiming for polite indifference. Her eyes sparked with amusement, amusement on his behalf, no doubt, dispelling any notion that she was anything less than ornery.

"Now you're gonna get it," he said, silky, soft and dangerous.

She squeaked and turned, darting away. Either the crowd of women believed he was a true danger to her or were in on the game because they massed, hiding her as she made her escape. John wove through them with difficulty. Suddenly each of them felt it necessary to reach out and present him with their wares, impeding his progress. When he was finally through the throng of humanity, Juniper was nowhere in sight.

He stood on the other side of the crowd, searching, stilling his senses, trying to use them to locate the lone girl who eluded him. He felt...he had no idea what he currently felt, nor did he actually care to find out. It was enough that Juniper was once again making him feel something unwelcome. And everything he felt was unwelcome, especially in regard to her. She frustrated him, more than anyone in recent or long-term memory. And yet...

"You might as well come out. I know you're here, and you know I'm going to find you."

When another piece of fruit landed on the back of his head, he whirled. Juniper stood at the edge of the jungle, leaning casually against a tree, tossing a mango in her palm. "Getting kind of rusty on those tracking skills, Major. Must be because of your advanced age," she yelled, cupping her hand around her mouth to be heard.

"Who taught you to throw like that?" he yelled in return. Unlike her, he had no need to cup his mouth. His voice boomed from so many years barking orders.

"I'm lookin' at him," she called.

He shouldn't grin at that, shouldn't encourage her—not that she'd ever needed encouragement to find trouble. But he couldn't seem to help himself. "Girl, you need a whoopin'," he called in return.

"Is that a threat or a promise?" she returned.

He took a step toward her. With a squeal, she tossed the mango in the air and disappeared into the thick foliage. John debated the merits of chasing her. He had too many things to do today, actual work for which he was being paid. But he was tempted, a little too tempted to pursue.

Slowly and with effort, he made himself turn away from the temptation that was Juniper Dunbar. And found everyone in the market staring at him with a matching grin of delight. He sighed. This little interlude had absolutely ruined his credibility as a staid army commander. On the other hand, it had likely done far more for community relations than any market day purchase he might have made. They seemed to be waiting on him to say something. He rolled his eyes and wound his finger around his ear. *"La mujer esta loca."*

One of the women clucked her tongue at him. *"El amor enloquece a las mujers." Love makes women crazy.*

John swiveled his attention back to the jungle. Of course Juniper didn't love him; she barely knew him. She was cuckoo for other reasons, by nature of being a Dunbar.

The woman had eased closer, getting the unexpected drop on him while his mind was on Juniper. She reached out and tapped his temple, drawing his attention back to her. *"Y los hombres tambien." And men, too.*

"No hay problema," he told her, holding up his hands in surrender. Not him, he would never be in love.

The woman grinned at him. *"Palabras famosas." Famous words.*

John walked back to camp shaking his head. Maybe all women were insane; maybe they were all in on it together. Good thing he was in no danger of succumbing to their ways.

CHAPTER 6

For two days, the situation with Juniper broiled in the back of The Major's mind. How on earth could he dislodge her? She didn't want to go and, if he were being honest, there was a teeny little part of him that didn't want her to. As hard as he had tried not to admit it, he had enjoyed catching up with Juniper Dunbar. Maybe it would be worth a visit to Alabama, next time he was in the states. He could put to bed some old ghosts. At the very least he could assuage the dim echo of guilt over his long absence.

Orders were orders, however. The area needed to be evacuated, and with good reason. Tensions had reached a boiling point. The Sandinistas were growing bolder, edging farther from their native Nicaragua into Honduras. Bankrolled and emboldened by the USSR, they were an ever-growing threat to Central America and, by extension, to the United States. The convoluted political minefield was why John and his team had been sent in, to be involved without making it look like they were involved. Secrecy was his specialty. Up front, they were there to support the Honduran peacekeeping effort. Behind the scenes, well, the less said, the better.

No matter how anyone cut it, it was the very last place a twenty two year old American botanist should be, kapok trees or no kapok trees. The entire area was like a box of tinder, ready to go up in flames at the slightest provocation. Juniper was in danger and had to go, like it or not.

The third time he visited her tent, her table was set for two, as if she'd been expecting him. "Bear," she declared, beaming as she unfurled herself from a chair, setting aside the giant tome she'd been reading.

"Juniper," he began. It was best to get it out of the way first before she got any notions about distracting him. He opened his mouth to continue when she once again preempted him.

"Did you know every girl in town had a crush on you?"

His mouth snapped together. "What?"

"I used to think about that a lot when I became a teenager, wondering what exactly they saw in you. Not that you weren't nice looking, of course you were. But so were a lot of boys from back home. Was it because you were aloof, a challenge? Or was it that quiet strength, that indelible Johnness?" Her head tipped, studying him.

"I don't, uh…" he scrubbed his hand over the back of his neck. Back then he'd had nothing but escape on his mind. Girls hadn't entered the picture. Ever, if he was truthful. It wasn't that he didn't like women. Of course he did. He liked their prettiness, their softness, their smell. It made a nice contrast from the sweaty soldiers usually around him. And when he pictured why he did what he did, who he fought for, it was always some nameless, faceless female. But he had always known that life wasn't for him—dating, relationships, marriage, fatherhood. John had been set apart, first by the events of his life, and then by his training. For that reason he had made himself the soldierest soldier of all. If there was a special training to further his skills or education, he took it. If there was an assignment too risky for the family men, he took that, too. If he were being honest, he hadn't expected to live to his current age. By all reasonable statistics he shouldn't have. He'd been close to death so many times he'd lost count. There had always been great comfort for him in knowing absolutely no one would mourn for him if he died.

"Juniper," he tried again, but again she preempted him as she steered him to the table and bade him sit down He did so and this time she plied him with some kind of pudding, its cool creamy texture sharp contrast to the day's heavy humidity. It was so pleasantly unexpected he stopped short and stared at, wondering how she managed it. No wonder the locals thought she was magic; maybe she was. He shook his head and attempted to try again.

"I was awfully sorry to hear about your Uncle Bailey," she said, tone soft and reverent.

John blinked, feeling oddly choked. After two years with the Dunbars, the State of Alabama finally found his only living relative, a salty old bachelor named Bailey Jones, his mother's great uncle. The old fellow was ancient, a crusty no-nonsense retired army guy who knew nothing about children. Everyone agreed John was better off with the Dunbars, everyone but John who longed to live with his uncle, if only for the escape it would provide. No more daily hugs at his uncle's house, no more clinging baby with blond mussy hair and sticky face, that was for certain. His uncle hadn't taken full custody, but he had kept a finger in John's life, pointing him toward the army and West Point, giving him a much-needed goal and directive. They corresponded often over the years, and John visited with him about once a quarter. And, despite the old man's standoffish stoicism, he had come to mean a great deal to John. They'd been as close as two uncommunicative men could be. It had been a painful blow when he died three months after John graduated West Point.

"Thank you," he said as his spoon scraped the bottom of the bowl. Somehow he had eaten all the pudding without saying what he came here to say. He took a breath.

"It hurts to lose people we love, leaves a hole," she mused.

He paused, regarding her with a frown. What could Juniper possibly know about loss? She, who had been so beloved by every member of her family. Their darling baby girl. It was a wonder she hadn't turned out spoiled. He opened his mouth to put her on blast.

"Have you been to your parents' grave?"

He blinked, shocked by the abrupt subject change. The Dunbars were big about visiting graves. John had never gotten it, but he had dutifully gone along four times a year to the cemetery where his parents were buried. Her parents would lay flowers. The whole family stood silent and reverent a moment, and then they would leave him alone to "say what he needed to say." He wondered if they realized he never said a word. Nice as it was, the whole ritual had seemed a bit bizarre to him.

"No, not once since I left."

"Hmm," she said. Even though she didn't say it, he could feel her disapproval.

"I don't go in for all that sentimental nonsense, Juniper."

"I know. I just..." she stared into space on her right. "If not their graves, where do you find them?"

He blinked at her. "I don't. You know how it ended. That's not something I care to revisit."

"What about all the years that came before the end?" she asked.

He scowled. "I don't revisit it. Ever. With anyone."

"Oh," she said, nodding sagely as if she had gained some cosmic insight into his soul.

Irritated now, he traded saucers with her, ate the remainder of her pudding, and then blinked at his newly empty bowl. In all his life, he was certain he had never done something so petty and immature. No doubt about it, Juniper Dunbar made him insane. He had the sudden vision of more visits like these. He would keep attempting to get a word in and she would keep diverting him, keep plying him with food, keep poking at his depths and old wounds he'd rather forget. He wouldn't, *couldn't* let that happen. Calm now, he dabbed his lips with the napkin and stood. Juniper watched him curiously, a smile of amusement on her face. When he reached for her, she put her arms up, a repeat of so many scenes when they were kids. Except now he didn't tuck her cozily against his chest, trying to avoid her sticky jam hands. Now he hauled her up, tossed her over his shoulder, carried her to his Humvee, and tossed her inside.

CHAPTER 7

It took approximately twenty seconds for Juniper to realize she was being kidnapped and twenty five for her to start fighting like a wet cat. First she tried bailing out of the moving car, but, knowing her as he did, John had been prepared for that. The tank-like vehicle was rigged so only he could open the doors, in case he needed to transport a prisoner. When escape didn't work, she set on him, pouncing so that he swerved, hit a rut, and almost flipped the vehicle.

He slammed on the brakes, putting out a hand to keep her from barreling through the windshield. "I'll tie you. Is that what you want?"

"What I want," she repeated, enraged. "What I want? Are you insane? What I want is to be treated with dignity and respect, not like a piece of property. What I want is to go back to my tent and keep working."

Assured the threat was over now and she had moved on to ranting, he dropped his arm and righted the vehicle, getting them back on the path. There were no roads in these parts, only clearings that had been worn by villagers and animals. And now the US Army. Too late he realized she had stopped talking. He turned in time to see her sink her teeth into his bicep.

"Confound," he yelled, yanking his arm away and subduing her in one swift motion. "Do you sharpen your teeth?" He mashed her against the seat, keeping all of her body in check with his.

"Take me back," she demanded, furious.

"No," he said coolly. He had been in plenty of hand-to-hand combat situations before, too many to number, but always with a man. He was unprepared for the difference in subduing Juniper. She was so…soft. So little. He eased his grip, suddenly afraid he might hurt her, if he hadn't already. "Are you okay?"

She blinked at him, confused. "What?"

He eased farther away. "I didn't hurt you, did I?" He had the sudden vision of his mother, bruised, broken, and had to fight a wave of revulsion. He moved back to his position behind the steering wheel and sucked a deep breath.

"Of course you did," she said softly. His head whipped in her direction, noting her frown, arms crossed stiffly over her chest.

"What hurts?" Her arm? Her ribs? Her neck?

"Everything. You have to take me back. My work is my world, it's everything. I'm in the critical phase."

With effort, he refrained from rolling his eyes. "You shouldn't be so dramatic."

She made a little sound, somewhere between a gasp and a growl, and it was all he could do not to smile. Juniper was cute. Juniper angry was downright adorable. She thought she was so tough. She had no idea what tough was, nor should she ever. "You kidnapped me and you think I'm the dramatic one," she ground out.

"I gave you ample warning," he said.

"Ample warning of what? You don't get to boss people around, to take over their lives and make decisions for them," she said.

"Actually, I do," he said, tapping the insignia on his shirt.

"I am not in the army. I'm a private citizen. I have rights."

"You're not a Honduran citizen," he pointed out.

"No, but I have the country's permission to be here."

"Doesn't matter. Our mission preempts everything else. Besides, it's not like you can never come back. Let this blow over, let us get it settled."

"It doesn't work that way. Time is a critical factor," she said.

"Okay," he said, unconcerned. In his mind it was so easy to understand. Why couldn't she see it that way? This was why he had nothing to do with women. Their complete lack of logic baffled him.

"You think your work is more important than mine," she accused.

"Let me think about it, yes. Do you even understand what is going on here? How many people could be killed if this thing comes to a head the way it's going? I am here to save lives. You are here to look at leaves."

"That…that is not…Oooh." She faced forward and forced a breath. When she spoke again, she was calmer. "What do you think I hope to gain from studying kapok trees?" Before he could begin to think of an answer, she answered for him. "Did you know their fibers are ultra absorbent, that they show promise as being used to treat trauma wounds, wounds like those sustained in war? Did you know the kapok tree is highly medicinal, that it shows promise of being used to slow bleeding, lower fevers, stop seizures? Do you really think I would risk my life to look at leaves under a microscope? This is work that could potentially help millions of people, and no one else is doing it."

He didn't know all that, and he *had* imagined her staring at leaves under a microscope, had never taken into account the larger implications of her work. But… "The order came from the top, Juniper. It's not up to me. You have to go."

"Like this? Without so much as a toothbrush? Without all my…" her voice broke and she sucked a breath. "Without all my pictures, my personal effects?"

He squinted, staring hard at the makeshift path. Had he done the wrong thing? It had seemed so clear-cut in her tent. She wouldn't leave; he had to make her leave. He gave a decisive little nod. He was right, she was wrong. "You wouldn't go, kept dodging me with your stall tactics. I didn't want it to be like this, but you forced my hand."

"You used your size to kidnap me, and you say I'm the one who forced your hand," she pointed out.

"You'll be fine," he assured her. "I'll have someone drive you to the

Honduran base. They'll keep you safe until you can get a flight out. I'll have someone pack your things and ship them. This is what's best; this is what's safest."

"Since when are you so all-fired concerned with safety? That's not the John I remember."

"It's been fourteen years. I've grown up."

"No," she said, shaking her head hard. "You've become…"

He braced himself. "What?" He'd heard it all before—cold, hard, robotic, aloof, heartless.

"A stranger," she said softly, then pressed her lips together, forced her gaze to the window, and didn't speak again.

John faced forward, tight-fisting the steering wheel. All the things people had called him over the years, some of them horrible, and yet that one nondescript word from Juniper Dunbar somehow hurt the most. He wondered why that was.

CHAPTER 8

She wouldn't look at him again, wouldn't say goodbye as he handed her off to someone to drive her to the base. She couldn't know that he hand selected one of the men he trusted most, a responsible family man who would keep her safe, who wouldn't bother her by trying to flirt.

"They'll get you home safely after you reach the base," he tried. She kept her face averted, arms crossed, lips pressed tightly together. "Probably be able to catch a flight tomorrow or the next day. There are a lot of transports going in and out these days." Nothing. The silence annoyed him because it made him feel…well, that was just it. It made him feel. He didn't like to feel, and he especially didn't like to feel what he now felt—guilt. He was doing the right thing. He knew it down to his core. He was keeping her safe, and that was what was most important. The area might soon be a war zone. Young pretty girls would be bandied about like trading cards. He had knowledge of what they'd do to her, knowledge she should never share. It was his duty to keep her safe, both as a man and as a soldier. But if she would look at him, say something, offer a smile or even eye contact, he'd feel some measure of peace, of closure. He had never needed those things before, but he hadn't dealt with someone like Juniper before, someone he'd known from early days.

"Someday you'll understand this is for the best," he tried. Still nothing except... He tilted his head, squinting. Was that...yes, a lone tear trickled down her cheek. It took everything in him not to wipe it away, not to reach out, draw her close, and make her understand. He was doing this for her own good, why couldn't she see that? And, more importantly, why did he care that she was upset? Orders were orders. It never bothered him before who he had to trample to carry them out. He tapped the car and gave the driver a nod. The man had questions, John could see them. This was the first bit of humanity his men had likely ever seen in him. More than a few of them were staring at him, watching his exchange with Juniper. He should get it together, resume his stern exterior. Instead he stood still and watched the Jeep until it was long out of sight. And then slowly, heavily, made his way into his tent. *Work,* he thought, stretching the kinks in his neck. *I need to work.*

But he didn't. He sat staring into space, his mind unable to focus. Maybe if he packed up some of her things, had them ready to go, it would make things easier. There were people he could send to do such a mundane task, at least a half dozen of them. But somehow he knew he needed to be the person to pack her personal effects, to make certain they were handled with care.

He bounded back to the Humvee and returned to Juniper's camp, feeling oddly bereft to be there without her. *What is wrong with you?* he questioned himself. He hadn't felt this way since...ever. It wasn't as if he and Juniper were close, wasn't as if he'd kept in contact with her or anyone from home the last fourteen years. He hadn't seen her since she was an eight-year-old child. She was still a child. A twenty two year old little upstart who thought she was big stuff because she was on assignment in the jungle. He pictured her face as it had looked that first day she turned and realized it was him, the surprise in her eyes, the warm light of welcome. Sharp contrast to the way she went away —sad, angry, dismayed. *Hurt.* No, not hurt. He refused to believe that. He hadn't done anything to hurt her. All he had done was his job.

Maybe his earlier prediction had come true and Juniper was spoiled now. How else to explain her overt reaction to not getting her way? She was pouting, like the child she was. In turn, he was disturbed at her petulance. Her parents had been indulgent, too free with their emotions, too liberal with personal freedom. Allowing their kids to run wild at all hours of the day or night, him included, all in the name of learning. *We want our kids to thirst for knowledge,* they had famously declared when they gave John the choice to keep going to school on his own or learn from home with the others. Of course he had chosen to homeschool. He had hated school. And then… Well, if he were being honest, then he had loved it, had loved being able to research topics that captured his interest. And almost everything had captured his interest. He had become a great reader after he lived with the Dunbars, investing himself in classics he otherwise wouldn't have espoused.

But even if he was willing to admit there was some merit in their style of education, he always felt they'd lacked discipline. And now that lack was being played out in Juniper who threw a fit, just because she'd been routed from her camp in the middle of a warzone. Why was it so hard for her to understand she had been in danger? *She's too dratted soft,* he thought with a disgusted shake of his head. *Too vulnerable, too breakable.* If an insurgent got hold of her they… He had to break off that line of thought before he snapped the steering wheel. That wouldn't happen now. She'd be out of harm's way. In a couple of days she'd be back in the states. With her fiancé. They would probably get married now, as they should. A woman like Juniper shouldn't be alone. She was too soft, too vulnerable, too adorable too…

He broke off his thoughts again and stormed into her tent.

It was a large tent, more of a yurt, likely paid for by whichever university sent her. It wasn't secure, of course, but it was spacious, especially for a lone woman, and it would have done a good job of keeping the mosquitos out, along with any jaguars that might otherwise try to overcome their inherent shyness and attack.

The cabinet by her bed likely contained all her personal items. He moved there now and crouched, opening it with a yank. Everything wooden tended to swell in the high humidity. There were girly things —lotions, sprays hair tonics. He gathered them and set them in the box he'd brought. Next came a small decorative box marked "pictures." Unable to contain his curiosity, he opened the box and came face to face with a picture of himself. Unsurprisingly, the Dunbars had also been into pictures. Seemingly every day they took a picture of something or other the family was doing. And with such a large family, there had been a lot of celebrations—birthdays, Christmases, Easters. The photos hadn't stopped there, nor had the festivities. They celebrated every time someone lost a tooth, every Veteran's Day, President's Day, anything and everything that could be cause for jubilation had been observed. The picture in question looked like it had been some sort of patriotic celebration. John knew because he wore a red t-shirt, no doubt selected by his foster mother specifically for the occasion. And in his arms was Juniper, bedecked in a red, white, and blue dress, chubby arms around his neck and clinging tight, cheek pressed against his. As usual, her cheek had smears of something pink, ice cream, perhaps? John looked as though he tried to pull away, probably to avoid getting it on himself. Juniper had no such compunctions, full in on her hug, messy cheek mashed firmly to his clean one. It was a metaphor for their entire childhood—Juniper clinging, John trying to wriggle away.

He stared at the picture feeling…oh, how was he supposed to assign a name to every blasted emotion? He felt something, and wasn't that enough? The problem was, he didn't *want* to feel anything, didn't want to remember how it had been when he was part of the Dunbar family, at least peripherally. He had cut ties with them, with everyone, with everything. Ever since his uncle Bailey died, he had considered himself an orphan in every way, completely untethered.

But he wasn't, not really. There was a family who had loved him, who had raised him from twelve to eighteen, who had taken him in when he had nowhere else and lavished him with affection, attention, and understanding. And even though he hadn't wanted those things— then or now—that didn't negate the fact that they'd given them and given them freely. And how had he repaid them? By disappearing.

Had he ever even thanked them? They had received a stipend from the state for his care, but it hadn't been nearly enough to cover all the food he ate, the clothes he wore, the presents he received for every blasted occasion. They had been generous with him, overtly so, and he had shoved that generosity in their faces. His conscience smote him, he who had tried hard to live above reproach, with honor and character, had done a bad thing to people who did nothing more than love him.

And they *had* loved him. He never doubted that. They had never once made him feel like an outsider, never less than a part of their family.

When this assignment was over, he would make amends. He would go home and thank the Dunbars for all they had done on his behalf. Maybe they hadn't understood him, hadn't met him on a level where he could accept and appreciate their care, but they hadn't been stingy or cruel with him, had only ever wanted the best for him. It wasn't their fault he was already dead and closed off in all the ways that mattered by the time he arrived at their doorstep. Maybe by the time he got home, Juniper would be married. He could meet her husband, make certain he approved of the man. *What will happen if I don't approve of him?* He wondered but found no answer and that was disquieting for reasons he didn't understand.

Maybe that was what was so frustrating, what had always been frustrating about his involvement with the Dunbars. He neither wanted nor understood any of the emotions they evoked in him. He knew they were good people, knew they were caring and kind. But he hadn't wanted their goodness, nor their care and kindness. It was the reason he had wanted to live with his uncle instead of them. Bailey would have left him alone, would have let him stew in his isolation.

He would never be like other people, his father assured that when he murdered his mother and then himself before John's eyes. There was no possible healing from that, no chance to recover. John understood it instinctively, almost as soon as it happened. His father might as well have killed him that night because something inside him died regardless. He could never be a real part of a family. His life with the

Dunbars had proved that. Happiness and love had churned around him and he had watched it like swirling fog, always unable to reach out and grasp it, to hold it to himself, to let it become part of him. If he was ever going to heal, to become whole, it would have happened then, from twelve to eighteen when he had been steeped in love and affection, so much he was almost drowning in it. Instead he'd become more reserved, more distant, more resolved in his separateness.

He wished he could figure out a way to explain to Juniper, but it was impossible. To do so would only further what she saw as a bond between them. There was a part of him that wanted her to understand and a part of him that didn't. Telling her would extend his misery, would bring him closer to realizing what he could never have. Not telling her was like ripping off a bandage, a quick sting of pain, soon forgotten. Knowing and being known by someone was another luxury he could never afford. Long ago he had accepted the life he now lived. He was a solider, that was all. His life was about duty, nothing else. And that was okay. More than okay. He had purpose, great purpose, and that brought him more satisfaction than anything ever had.

Going to Juniper's camp had been the right decision, had provided the closure he needed. He would send her effects and then, when things settled, he would visit the Dunbars and give them his thanks. He owed them that much, probably more. Knowing them, they would want to stay in contact, would want to invite him to all the family gatherings henceforth. He would give his apologies and explain it was out of the question. His life was not his own; he belonged to the army in all the ways.

With a definitive nod, he picked up the box of Juniper's things and headed back to the Humvee. He felt almost cheerful now. The last few days with Juniper were a blip. He would forget her and return to how it was, how it had always been.

His mind once again clear, he drove to camp, ready to work. A queue of nervous looking soldiers stood outside his tent, nudging each other. It was a familiar gesture to The Major. *You tell him, no you tell him.* Had he ever been that frightened of a superior as these men were? He couldn't remember, but he didn't think so.

"Is there a problem?" he asked as he stepped out of the vehicle.

Once again the men traded glances. One of them cleared his throat and took a tentative step forward. But that seemed to be as much resolve as he possessed. He stood still, blinking at John, mouth agape.

"Speak up, soldier," John barked and the man flinched like he'd been hit. He cleared his throat and tried again.

"Sir, we received word there was an ambush."

Quickly, John's mind flicked through all the hotspots in the country, already arranging strategy to counteract the fallout. "Where?"

The men traded glances again. John couldn't understand their odd reticence until another of them piped up, one he'd sent to try and send Juniper packing. "Sir, they took her, they took Juniper."

CHAPTER 9

Nothing in his life had ever prepared John for the way hearing those words would make him feel. After ten years in the military and four at West Point, war was finally personal. It had never occurred to him it could be, mostly because he had no people. But he had Juniper. However tangential she was to his life, she had at one time been central to him, to his wellbeing, even when he hadn't wanted her to be. She had been the person he spent ten hours a day with, however reluctantly on his part. From the moment she woke to the moment she went to bed, she had only wanted John. She had been foisted on him, shoved into his care—a standoffish, singular teenager. Why her parents thought they'd be a good match was anybody's guess, but somehow they had worked. He had tempered her wild exuberance; she had bolstered his sullen melancholy. Being too introspective or morose hadn't been possible when he'd been doing his best to keep a toddler alive, despite her repeated attempts to ignore all danger and do away with her little life.

And now once again, at the ripe age of thirty two, he found himself in the role of her protector and rescuer. Only this time it was his fault she was in trouble. Reasonably he shouldn't, couldn't have been the one to leave camp and drive her to the base. He was in charge of the entire operation; he couldn't walk away to shuttle a civilian like an overqualified taxi service. But somehow he knew that if he'd been the one to go, Juniper would now be safe. It was the same way he knew he had to be the one to go get her because, reasonably and without conceit, he was the best.

So when his men told him of her kidnap, he didn't explode at them like they probably expected, didn't put anyone on blast or toss anyone from his sight, as he sometimes did when he became too disgusted with their weakness or incompetence. Instead he strode calmly past them, unloaded his gun, and locked it in his drawer. Then he pulled out his pack and started to prepare.

In the second drawer, he reached for the weapons he'd take along —a machete he'd bought at a local market, a knife he pulled out of an East German operative's gut, and a gun he won in a poker game with a Soviet operative. It absolutely would not do to leave a trace, to be able to assign blame for the coming carnage on the United States Army. That was why he needed weapons that couldn't be traced to him. The Soviet gun was clunky and unrefined, but it would work as it was supposed to. And it was likely he wouldn't need it anyway. John was an expert shot, but his other skills made it so that he rarely had to fire his weapon. Those skills were the reason he was sent the places he went—to get in and get the job done undetected. For a couple of years he'd done wet work—killing people the army told him needed killed. Being an assassin had been okay, but there hadn't been much challenge in it. As he matured, he realized he enjoyed the planning of a mission as much as the execution. It was like viewing a giant chessboard and being able to arrange the pieces. He had an eye for strategy, for, well, for war. Somehow he always knew what the enemy was going to do and how best to disable them. So far that deadly combo of intuition and skill had led him to success. And now it would help him find and rescue Juniper. He wouldn't allow himself to believe it might already be too late; she was more valuable to them alive. What concerned him was how much they could do to her before he found her.

Rage attempted to seep in, but he wouldn't let it. Emotion was a weakness he couldn't allow. He would find her and make her well, no matter what. With that thought in mind, he reached into the box he'd brought from her camp and added her toothbrush and toothpaste to his pack.

His sergeant was one of the men standing outside his tent. "You're in charge until I return," he said, which was probably an extraneous thing to say, of course the sergeant was in charge in his absence. But they seemed to be waiting on him to make some sort of statement. An intention of his imminent return seemed the safest option.

"Sir," the sergeant surprised him by speaking. "Do...do you need help? We could all go?"

John surveyed the men feeling...what? Grateful? Touched? Annoyed? He cleared his throat. "I appreciate the offer, Sergeant, but this is bound to be a delicate operation, one best handled alone." With one final nod, he hopped in the Humvee and sped away, following the same route the earlier car had taken.

He had no trouble finding the disabled Jeep in the roadway. It had already been stripped of its parts. He should have had someone drive him this far, so the same wouldn't happen to the Humvee, not that they'd have such an easy time of it. They'd need a saw or welding kit to do the same thing that had been done to the Jeep. There was some comfort in that, he supposed. Besides, the men who did the earlier job were long gone now and likely wouldn't be back.

He hopped from the truck, shouldered his pack, and disappeared into the jungle, pausing to listen and observe. John had been a tracker long before he was a soldier. His father had taught him how, one of the only good things he'd passed along. He knew how to read the signs, observe the earth and follow prey. It was a skill that used to fascinate Juniper. Together they had spent their days following deer deep into the woods, her on his back when the terrain became too rough. Despite his earlier teasing, she *had* been surprisingly good at being still and silent, intent on watching the birds or animals they followed. She could be prattling endlessly, as she often did, but when John put his finger to his lips, she went mute, waiting, watching.

Strange how easily he had forgotten all that. For six years she'd been the biggest part of his life, but he had cut her out of it with knife-like precision, the same way he cut out everything when he became a soldier. He was the job, only the job. Nothing that came before mattered, or so he thought. But now, as he advanced through the jungle following an invisible path, the memories came pouring back. Far from being painful as he thought they might, they felt like healing oil, a salve to all his broken pieces. He'd been part of a family once, a good one, no matter how strange and eccentric they might have been.

Dustin Dunbar, Juniper's father, had been a fulltime college professor once, until he retired and devoted himself to editing academic journals. It was a profession that allowed him to make his own schedule, to work from home and be with his family. But he never lost his love of teaching, his joy of discovery. He had passed that along to all of his children and John, too. John's own mother had a love of learning, even though she hadn't received much education. She used to take John to the library and pile a massive stack of books for both of them. And then when she finished reading all of her books, she would read all of his. His father, a manly man who eschewed softness in any form, never made fun of them for their love of reading. It seemed to be the one sacred thing he wouldn't touch, and John had come to treasure it as something important, a lesson that was furthered by his time at the Dunbars'. Dustin Dunbar had been an impassioned teacher; in John he'd found an eager pupil, if nothing else. He might not have been receptive to all the love and affection they tried to heap on him, but he had been ravenous for an education. It was that desire to learn and excel that earned him a spot at West Point, where he graduated among the top in his class.

Another thing I need to thank them for, he thought. He had already compiled quite a list. It was his Uncle Bailey who pointed him toward West Point and set it as a goal, but it was the Dunbars who made it possible, who patiently encouraged him to take his studies seriously at a time when it would have been easy to languish in his trauma. When he thought about it, so many people had whispered into his life as a boy, so many people had a hand in guiding him toward success. He might have ended in ruin, in prison or, worse, dead. Instead he'd been given a purpose, a mission, and been given the tools to succeed. *What are you doing to repay all that?* His insistent inner voice whispered, pricking his conscience once more. To whom much is given, much is expected, but what was he doing to begin to repay his debt? Whose life did he influence? His subordinates were terrified of him, but he didn't think that counted as influence. He'd saved people, successfully pulled them through missions and kept them alive when the odds were greatly against them. But that was his job. It had nothing to do with him as a person. When he thought about it in those terms, he couldn't think of one person he had steered on course, mentored, challenged to grow and keep learning the way Dustin and Bailey had for him. And that was a shame, a deep and lasting shame. John was in a position of great power. Shouldn't he use that for good? To cultivate future leaders and men of character?

Suddenly an insurgent emerged from the jungle to his right, yelling, arms held aloft as he charged. And then he was on the ground, John's hand around his neck, keeping him contained like an errant calf. These were the times he knew he wasn't normal. Other men, men he'd known, men he'd trained, felt adrenaline surges in these moments as their fight-or-flight instincts kicked in. John felt nothing. Not fear, not elation, not horror—nothing. Just a calm directive in his brain, telling him what to do in order to succeed. Pin the man. Get the information. Decide whether or not to dispose of him.

"Donde esta la mujer?" His words were a silken whisper in the man's ear, soft yet full of so much threatened retribution the man began to tremble.

"No sé," the man's panicked voice trembled out of him, over and over again, pleading. *"No sé."*

John's grip tightened on his neck. His thumb pressed the middle of his throat, finding the proper spot. One twist and it would all be over. His eyes must have told the man how imminent his death was because he began to blubber.

"Donde esta la mujer?" John repeated it lower, slower, a snake gearing up for a strike.

"Este, la llavaron al este. Acampar."

East. To their camp. John would reach them before they arrived. He had to because if they reached their camp with her... His hand tightened on the man's throat again, and for the first time in his life he began to feel something as he stared at the man. Something bad. *Rage.* "Did you hurt her?" he demanded. The man blinked at him. The "soldiers," such as they were, were nothing more than a ragtag band of villagers who'd had enough poverty and decided to try something else. Uneducated, they were no less dangerous because they had an ideology. But John was a thousand times better trained than the man —who was really little more than a boy—beneath him. So he eased his grip and tried again. *"La lastimaste?"*

The man's eyes widened in panic. *"No. No, señor. Lo juro."* *I swear it.*

John felt something had been lost in translation. He didn't need to know if the man personally hurt her, he needed to know if Juniper was still unharmed. But then he realized he likely wouldn't get the truth from the terrified man. Once men started to release the fetid sweat of fear, they'd say anything to keep alive. The best course of action was to find Juniper and see for himself if she was okay. And if she wasn't...

The man made a sound beneath him and John realized he was choking him to death. He loosened his hold and the man gulped air as John had a quick mental debate. There was no reason to kill the boy and extra casualties would conjure questions, might create complications John didn't need. He could leave him unconscious long enough for John to get to his camp, but what if he rallied to come help his comrades? John had no idea how many there were, but the less, the better. *Alive,* John decided, but the man's hand made a sudden lunge for his weapon. It was the last move he'd ever make. Training kicked in and John eliminated the threat in seconds, shouldered his pack, and walked away without a backwards glance or hint of remorse.

CHAPTER 10

The jungle was thick and heavy, but John was determined. And such was his luck that he didn't have to use his machete. The band of rebels had already cleared a path for him. All he had to do was follow. He wondered why that was. Did they think no one would come for the woman they stole? Did they believe they were safe from the army's retribution? Probably. From their point of view, she was only one little woman, not much use to the United States Army. What they failed to realize was that, as a United States citizen, she had their full protection. John would have retrieved her regardless. For anyone else he would have sent a team of men, and it probably would have been enough. But this was Juniper Dunbar and nothing less than John's special brand of soldiering would do. For Juniper he needed the best, he needed perfection. That meant he'd do it himself, the first time he'd personally been in the field in half a decade.

For any other reason, at any other time, he would have been glad to get back in the field. Excited, even. Ops were fun. Even the ones like this where he trekked through the jungle in impossible heat, drenching his clothes and pack. Physical needs didn't seem to affect John like other men—hunger, fear, thirst, heatstroke, dehydration. He seemed impervious to them all, another thing that set him apart from the others, that had guaranteed his rise through the ranks. It was as if he'd been programmed at birth to be a soldier, if not at birth then by life events. For better or worse, his father had trained him well for the life he now led. Whatever his father left out, West Point filled in. John was a soldier, irrevocably and forever, inside and out. He ate, breathed, slept and dreamed military life. While other men couldn't wait to get home, John dreaded leave, always feeling at loose ends and antsy. While other men counted down to retirement, it loomed on John's horizon like a nightmare. Somehow he knew if he ever stopped working, he would drop dead immediately, his purpose complete. Because without the army, what did he have? Nothing. Absolutely nothing.

The tracks were becoming fresher. John sharpened his focus, dispelling all other thoughts. The Major had become a predator now, stalking his prey before the final pounce.

When he was near enough, he climbed a tree for an aerial view of the camp. Five men, heavily armed with Soviet machine guns, proving their enemy's influence. They were Sandinistas, and yet John was relieved. If they had been Contras, armed with American guns, the situation would have been even more complex. As it was he could categorize them as enemies, of the state, of Honduras and, as of this moment, himself personally. That was a new one on John. He was used to not having any personal involvement. The chain of command told him who to abolish; John didn't need to know why. As his rank grew, the chain grew shorter. Currently there were few links between him and the president. Someday if he stayed on his current trajectory he would likely report to the president directly. It was his goal in life to be that man, to be in the top brass. Why? He couldn't say for certain. It wasn't for the glory, he wanted none of that. Not even for the power, he'd seen how easily it could corrupt. Maybe he merely wanted to stand in the gap, to be a buffer between the men who made the decisions and the men who were forced to carry them out. If there was one thing that came close to pushing John's emotional hot button, it was politicians who disregarded the lives of the men who served in their defense.

But now, as he sat in the tree and observed the rough camp, Washington was far away. Everything was far away but Juniper Dunbar and these men.

One of them emerged from the coarse tent, scowling. He spoke to his comrade, and John strained to listen. *"Ella quiere un coco."*

John knew better than to make a sound, but it was all he could do to subdue his laughter. *She wants a coconut.* If he'd had any doubts about how Juniper was holding up, they evaporated. Apparently her charm worked the same on the Sandinistas as it did his men. A coconut. *Oh, Juniper.* He didn't move, barely even blinked, but inside he smiled, secretly proud of his girl. His girl? Only years of training kept him from scowling over the errant thought. *Not my girl.* Never had she been his girl. She had only ever been his albatross, his annoyance, his burden to bear, trudging her on his back like a pack mule through the hot Alabama woods, trying to keep her from becoming alligator food, from becoming snake bit, bee stung. If he'd been more superstitious, he might have thought she was the devil in child form, sent to plague him. As it was, he'd seen through her parents' well-intentioned plan. *Let's pair our most exuberant child with the most recalcitrant one. Maybe she'll work her magic on him. And if not, at least she's out of our hair.* He had to hand it to the Dunbars, they'd been smart. If he were a parent, he'd probably do the same thing they'd done. Too bad for them it hadn't worked, at least on his end. He'd done plenty to keep Juniper alive and safe, but she'd done nothing to plumb the depths of his unfeeling, sealed off heart.

You're here, aren't you? An annoying little voice whispered in his head. What was worse was that the voice sounded a lot like Juniper's.

Shut up, he scolded the voice. He had work to do.

He narrowed his eyes on the two men speaking outside the tent.

"Why a coconut?" the second man asked.

"I split her lip when I hit her. She said it's good for healing skin."

John wasn't aware he'd moved until he was moving toward them. By the time the one closest to the tent realized his friend was now gone, it was too late for him, too.

John's hand hesitated on the tent flap. The urge to check on

Juniper, to assure himself she was alive and well, was almost over-powering. But he needed to take care of the other three men before he allowed himself to be reassured. *Disable the threat, then check the hostage.*

With more effort than he would have thought possible, he turned away from the tent and headed toward the other men.

One man eked out a small sound as he fell. It worked as a warning to the others who caught sight of John and began to charge toward him together, machine guns fumbling in fingers that were suddenly too thick. John could practically hear what they were thinking as their fear and glee mingled together. *An American soldier in their camp, and he was alone with no discernable weapon. What a prize he would be!*

He stood still as they advanced, after assuring himself they were far too slow on the draw to do any damage to him or Juniper by mistake. And then it was as if they both realized at once there must be some reason he didn't move, some reason he stood there, awaiting their advance. Or maybe it was his placid expression that warded them off. He didn't smile. That would be psychotic. It wasn't as if he enjoyed what was about to happen. It was merely that he'd long ago accepted killing as part of his duty. Sometimes he could protect and serve without any casualties. Other times, like now when Juniper's health and safety hung in the balance, there would be the opposite outcome.

The two Sandinista's stopped short, bracing their weapons across their chests as they regarded him.

"What are you doing here?" the first one asked in badly broken English. John decided to rescue them both by answering in Spanish so there'd be no mistakes.

"Vine por la chica." I came for the girl.

"Alone?" the second man said, incredulous. His eyes began to skitter the edges of the camp, certain backup must be hiding in the jungle.

John said nothing because he owed them nothing, not an answer, not the truth.

"You can't have her," the first man said, regaining some bravado as he remembered his gun and leveled it at John's chest.

"She's ours now," the second man agreed, and he also leveled his gun on John.

For his part, John felt a small measure of relief. He would have killed them regardless, but it went against the grain to take out two men without a fight, especially when his skills made the playing field so uneven.

"Russian triggers are sticky," he warned them, and then dove between them as they began to fire—slow, too slow to hit him. One of their triggers did stick and the man cursed, the curse ending on a scream when John sliced through his Achilles tendon with his left hand, slicing the Achilles tendon of the man on his right simultaneously.

The one on his right reached wildly for his injured leg, spraying the ground inches from John with bullets in his haste to ease the pain. John dodged out of the way and disarmed the man, snapping his wrist free of its socket as he fell. He jammed the gun and used the butt of it to slam into the other man's nose.

A few seconds later it was over, the camp was silent. John wasn't even winded. He closed his eyes, listening, observing with his tracker instincts. For now, no other soldiers were nearby. How long that would last he couldn't say. This camp had been a splintered portion of a much larger one. The Sandinistas were breaking apart in order to maintain cover as they slid into Honduras. There were more out there, waiting. Hoping for their chance to attack. The sooner they began to move, the better.

He faced the tent and took a breath. Now that the danger was on pause, he felt a strange sense of foreboding he couldn't put a name to. It was time to retrieve Juniper, to get her out of here, to carry her to safety. There was no time for hesitation, and yet he dithered, he who never vacillated or dallied now stood shifting from foot to foot, as uncomfortable as any of the green pups who paused anxiously outside his tent. And *that* was the mysterious something he hadn't been able to put his finger on. He was afraid. Of Juniper Dunbar. Afraid she'd still be angry at him, afraid she'd blame him for her kidnap, afraid she might be so hurt beyond repair he might lack the skills to put her back together again.

Patting the book in his pocket for reassurance, he sucked up his courage and took a step toward the tent.

CHAPTER 11

She sat on the floor of the tent, hands and feet bound in front of her, a gag tied around her bruised and bleeding mouth. One eye was also purple and puffy. Immediately John's brain ran to all the damage a man's fist could do to the delicate occipital area, especially on a woman.

He knelt in front of her, his knife making short work of the binds, and then they inspected each other a few beats in silence. Tentatively, his fingers reached out and probed her eye, soft and gentle. Slowly, as if seeking permission or uncertain of his welcome. She winced but didn't shy away. His thumb smoothed the rim of her eye, feeling for cracks. Satisfied the injury wasn't serious, he began to take stock, not of her, but of himself and his feeling of unease. Something was wrong, something was missing, and it took him a moment to realize what it was. *Her dimple.* Juniper dimpled when she smiled and even dimpled in anger. At this moment her face was flat and dimple free and he finally understood why: she was afraid. He had never seen her afraid before, not once. Not of heights nor falling from them, not of snakes or bats or spiders, not of him or anyone else they'd encountered. Understanding this made him do a thing he hadn't done since his mother died—he reached out both arms and gave her a hug.

The motion felt rusty and unused, so much that he wondered if he was doing it wrong, if maybe he'd forgotten how the last twenty years without. When Juniper remained motionless and unresponsive, he was sure he'd messed it up. But no, she was merely surprised by the action. After a pause she leaned into him, melding her softness to his strength, resting her head on his shoulder. When she started to tremble, he sat and pulled her into his lap, his hand making clumsy passes over her hair.

"You're all right," he said with a softness he didn't recognize. His voice was always rough, never tender. Except with Juniper, apparently. He was so fascinated by the change in himself he repeated it. "You're all right, Juni."

She trembled violently a minute, as if she were pouring her fear into him, letting him absorb it so she could rid herself of it. At last she sagged in his grasp loose and exhausted, her body slack with spent adrenaline.

"I knew you'd come," she whispered.

He didn't reply because what could he say? That it had been his duty? It hadn't. He could have sent any of his men, a fact she'd easily recognize. When he thought about it, really thought about it, there was no rational reason he'd come for her, and that confounded him because rational thought was the foundation of his life. He scowled into the distance, not seeing the tent opposite, not seeing anything but his own confusion. Was their former connection enough to make him disregard the basic principles he'd based his entire career, his entire life on?

"We should go," he said, his voice regaining its former gruffness. "Can you walk?"

"If I say no, will you carry me?" She pulled away to gaze up at him and her dimple popped.

Juniper was back, his Juniper. *Not my Juniper, the real Juniper, the one with spunk and grit.* "If I say yes, will you fake an injury to make me prove it?"

Her lashes fluttered. "Why, Major Caruthers, was that a spark of humor?"

"Humor is a luxury a good soldier can't afford," he said.

"Humor's a necessity a good soldier can't do without," she returned.

"As if you'd know anything about being a soldier," he said.

"As if you'd know anything about humor," she countered, and he laughed, one sharp blast of laughter that took them both by surprise.

"Let's go, you imp, before more rebels find us."

"I bet you say that to all the girls."

"I do, in fact," he agreed, helping her stand. Seemingly the only time he ever encountered women was when he rescued one of them. And even then they shied away from him as if he were the enemy. Most women instinctively understood that he was fundamentally broken and they should stay away. Leave it to Juniper Dunbar to ignore the danger signals as usual. He paused, regarding her. "Your boyfriend doesn't beat you, does he?" What if she ignored danger signals with everyone? What if she had no instincts for self-preservation whatsoever?

"My fiancé, and he can't even bring himself to swat flies. He's a pacifist."

John choked.

She quirked an eyebrow at him. "You have a problem with pacifists?"

"No, I'd kill an enemy combatant to protect and defend them, same as anybody else. The fact that they wouldn't return the favor is on their conscience, not mine."

"Oh, boy," she muttered.

"What?" he asked when nothing else was forthcoming.

"You're gearing up for an old fashioned Dunbar debate, but I lack the energy to partake," she replied.

John grinned and realized it was true. The Dunbars were big into deliberation, taking different sides in order to sharpen points and play devil's advocate. Once John acclimated to their family dynamic and realized they weren't actually arguing or angry, he'd loved to partake.

"Let's shelve it for later," he said.

Juniper laughed and clasped his hand, giving it a squeeze. "I should have guessed your version of flirting would involve a healthy dispute."

He opened his mouth to tell her he hadn't been flirting, that he had never flirted with a woman in his life. Such behavior was frivolous and beneath him. But something held his tongue. The fact was Juniper was the person he'd known longer than anyone else in the world. If he couldn't tease and have fun with her, then maybe there really was something inherently wrong with him. Plus it was *Juniper*. She had never been serious for longer than three seconds in her life. Even in the midst of a kidnapping she took delight in teasing him.

"You should see what I do when I'm in love," he said, giving her hand a squeeze in return.

She laughed in delight, dimple popping impossibly deep. "I can hardly imagine. And guess what?" She swung their joined hands between them, smiling up at him with pure orneriness. Whatever was about to come out of her mouth would be filled with rottenness, he was sure.

"What?"

She stood on her toes and whispered in his ear. "Your accent's back."

"It is not," he argued, but he heard it, the slow drawl that could only be born from years in the Alabama backwoods. "Oh, for the love," he added, muttering. Now he'd have to work to get rid of it all over again before his men heard and began to circulate rumors that he was human, with a past and a people. And if they saw him with Juniper, they'd know for certain. She was his past; she was his people.

"Come on, you bothersome little kid." He said it in the same tone he used to say it, half exasperation, half amusement, and tugged her toward the encroaching jungle. And all of a sudden he felt the same way, too, a calming sense of peace, of belonging and togetherness. He had spent six years of his life with Juniper Dunbar as his constant companion, able to find solitude only when she was asleep. Being back there again after so many years didn't hurt his feelings, not even a little.

"**W**here are your glasses?"

They were still hand in hand, which was sort of ridiculous, considering how much John had to use the machete with his other hand. It was likely the rebels had cleared a path recently, but the jungle was always quick to reclaim its lost territory, sometimes within hours. They could probably go slightly faster if he could use both hands. But Juniper seemed to need the reassurance of human contact. She was that sort, the touchy-feely kind. All the Dunbars were. As a kid, all the extraneous touch used to drive him crazy. Only Juniper had been allowed to hang on him without him shying away and physically withdrawing. Strange how much some things hadn't changed. Despite the fourteen-year gap since the last time he saw her, and the fact she was no longer a child, he felt comfortable with her, physically and otherwise.

"You just now noticed they're missing? I remember when you were observant," she said.

"I remember when you weren't impertinent," he countered.

"No you don't," she returned.

"No I don't," he agreed. "So what happened?"

"They were lost in the tussle," she said. She squinted a little, remembering the feel of the glasses or the feel of the struggle, he couldn't be certain.

He stopped and took her chin between his thumb and finger, inspecting her again, anxious he might have missed something the first time. "What exactly happened?"

She swallowed hard and licked her split, now trembling lip. "Not too much. They weren't happy with my response to one of their suggestions about what to do with me. They hit me a couple of times."

"Is that the first time in your life you've ever been hit?" he asked.

She nodded, long, dewy lashes blinking slowly over inquisitive eyes as she peered up at him. "Please don't tell me I'll like it better the second time."

He barked a harsh laugh. "No. But at least you'd be prepared for it."

"There's no preparation for that," she said, fighting a grimace.

"It doesn't matter because it will never happen again," he vowed, tone solemn.

"I'd say you were being hyperbolic, but..." she motioned to the trail of carnage in their wake.

"I don't do hyperbole, Juni."

"Me neither," she said and he laughed again. "What?" she demanded.

"You ooze hyperbole and drama."

"I do not," she disagreed, becoming well and truly angry now. He could tell by the way her dimple winked up at him, as if in warning.

"You have always been the most dramatic of the Dunbar children."

For a second, hurt flashed in her eyes. "I was a child then. I'm not a child anymore, and I am not overly dramatic, nor prone to exaggeration. Do not confuse exuberance and passion with something else, merely because you're lacking both."

He didn't reply, merely kept walking in ascetic silence. John rarely argued back. If other men—or women—wanted to waste their energy on such a fruitless pursuit, it was nothing to him, merely one more thing out of his control.

Juniper stalked along beside him a few minutes in silence. She yanked her hand free of his grasp and he bit the inside of his cheek to stop his grin. He could feel her anger building and he wasn't certain which steamed more, the air around him or her fuming ire. Convinced she would burn herself out, he ignored her, a tactical mistake when she suddenly jumped on his back and tried to take him to the ground.

Not breaking stride, he kept walking, which enraged her further. She struggled harder. He pushed her hair out of his face and kept walking, fighting a chuckle. And then she bit him.

"Confound," he yelped and, reaching behind with one hand, yanked her forward. Instinctively her arms and legs wrapped around him as he pressed her to a tree, scowling.

Caught off guard by the intimate new position, they blinked at each other, faces a centimeter apart. "Why do you always resort to biting?" he whispered.

"Why do you always resort to ignoring me?" she whispered in return.

"It's impossible to ignore you," he said.

"Because I bite?" she guessed.

"No." Her hair was a tangle of curls gone wrong, nose and cheek smeared with dirt and blood, and he had never seen anything more lovely.

"When is the first time it happened to you?" she asked.

Her question made him realize he'd been staring at her lips. "What?"

"When is the first time someone hit you?" she asked.

"I can't remember that far back."

Her hand stroked gently on his face. "Your dad?"

"Yes."

"I'm sorry," she said.

"Why?"

"Because it happened to you, because it hurt you."

"It doesn't do to dwell on the past, to linger on past hurts."

"There's a difference between dwelling and acknowledgement. Have you ever dealt with your childhood?"

"Depends on what you mean by 'dealt'."

"Have you talked to anyone, a doctor?"

"No," he choked.

"Because you think you're too tough?"

"No, because I think I've already moved on."

"Huh," she said, her fingers still making a soothing trail around his face. The touch should annoy him. He was gritty with sweat and didn't especially like to be touched but, like a feral cat that finds unexpected enjoyment in human companionship, he remained still, melting into her touch, tension draining out of him.

"Why don't you have a girlfriend?" she asked.

"Because I'm a soldier."

"Lots of soldiers have girlfriends or wives. Some find time for both."

"I'm not that kind of soldier. I'm the job, only ever the job. I have no connection to anyone anywhere."

"I beg to differ," she said, giving him a squeeze.

"I don't want to be connected," he said.

Now it was her turn to regard him in silence he found disconcerting. He'd expected argument. "No comment?"

She shook her head.

"Why not?"

She shook her head again. He lowered his brows in frustration he couldn't begin to understand.

"Am I getting too heavy for you?" she asked.

"Juniper, I could hold you all day," he replied. Her weight was nothing compared to some of the things or people he'd had to carry.

"Really," she said in a tone that left him feeling even more baffled. Somehow he felt she'd gained the upper hand in their dynamic and he couldn't put his finger on how. Nor why it made him feel so...squeamish. All he knew was that it was time to go. He should put her down so they could resume momentum and get everything back to where it should be.

"Hey, Bear," she said softly.

"Hmm," he said, a deer in headlights now, never knowing what else she might say or do that could make him feel even more off kilter.

She rested her head on his shoulder and gave him a tight squeeze. "I really missed you."

He didn't reply, but he found himself squeezing her tightly in return.

CHAPTER 12

"Do you have friends?"

When their hug ended, they resumed their trek. Now Juniper seemed to be making a study of him, if the barrage of innocuous questions was any indication.

"I have one friend," John said. He could tell he'd surprised her, and he enjoyed the feeling. He had no idea why and added it to the mounting pile of confusion where Juniper was concerned.

"Tell me about him. Her?"

"Him. We met at West Point, his name is Ben."

"Is he like you?" she asked.

He darted her a glance. What did that mean, like him?

"A soldier's soldier, the job," she explained, deepening her voice and flattening her expression to mimic him. Despite himself, he smiled.

"No. People like him. He has grand aspirations that will probably succeed."

"Don't you have aspirations?" she asked.

"I suppose, but not the same as his. He wants it all: wife, family, glorious career."

"And what do you want?" she asked.

He opened his mouth to answer and found he couldn't. What *did* he want? A few days ago it had seemed so clear, and now it was as if he could see his goal across a long distance with a fog between them. That fog was Juniper, he knew. She was putting his head in a muddle, making him feel, remember, and question things. What did he want? To stay alive? To have successful missions? To make a lasting impact? On whom? For what reason? "To do my duty," he said at last, satisfied to have latched on to something. "To serve with honor."

"I guess since you've already done that, you've accomplished all your life's goals," she mused.

"That's not...I don't..." He grunted, annoyed. He was not a person who floundered, stuttered, or questioned himself. Juniper made him do all those. The more flustered he became, the happier she looked, annoying him further. "You take great delight in plaguing me."

"Since the moment we met," she beamed, squeezing the hand that was still joined to hers somehow. How was it possible to be trotting through the jungle of Honduras, Juniper tagging along behind him? So easily had he slipped into old habits, they might have been back home in Alabama. Any moment now he expected to stumble out of the woods and head home for supper, could almost taste the fresh biscuits and blackberry jam her mother set on the table every night. His mouth began to water, and that was so infuriatingly embarrassing he missed the vine he'd been aiming for and embedded his machete in a tree trunk instead.

"You seem a little tense," Juniper noted as he used both hands to yank the machete.

"I'm not tense. I don't get tense," he snapped.

"Hmm," she said, her placid tone a contrast to his sharp one.

"Confound," he exclaimed, using both hands to yank the stuck machete. It jerked free with a rebound, swinging hard to his right, exactly where Juniper was standing, slicing through her shirt like water.

For a stunned second they looked at each other, blinking in shock, then he dropped the machete and reached for her, tugging her shirt upward, ready to staunch the wound. His panic was so overwhelming and immediate it took him a moment to realize he didn't see the bloom of blood, the gaping entrails he expected. Frantic, his fingers smoothed over her skin, staunching a hole that wasn't there. She said his name three times before he finally responded.

"*Bear*," she yelled shaking him.

His head snapped up, his too big pupils unable to focus on anything but the vision in his head—Juniper, injured and bleeding, because of him.

"I'm fine," she said, tone soothing and gentle. "It barely touched me."

"It...it cut your shirt."

"I always hated this shirt," she said, and it was such a Juniper thing to say he expelled a sharp breath that was half laugh, half gasp.

"I thought I killed you," he said. His gaze fastened on her stomach as if still unable to believe he hadn't filleted her.

"No, look, you didn't even break the skin." She took his index finger and traced it over the line the machete had made, so faint it was barely pink. "You didn't hurt me. You would *never* hurt me."

The way she said it, with so much definitive authority, made him wonder if she was privy to the visions in his head—his mother, broken and bleeding at the hands of his father. "I...I might," he whispered, the confession leaking from him unbidden.

"Have you ever hurt a woman?" she asked.

"No." He paused. There had been female soldiers, female insurgents. "Not in that way, at least."

"See? You wouldn't," Juniper said, triumphant.

"I've never..." he paused and cleared his throat. "I don't get close to women."

Juniper digested that tidbit, blinking, then reached up and stroked the side of his face. "You would never hurt me, ever."

"You don't know that," he said.

"I know you."

He started to argue that she didn't know him, of course she couldn't, not after a fourteen year absence. But the truth was she did know him because she knew the one thing about him he kept hidden from everyone else. She knew his beginning, the shameful truth of his parentage, his father's brutality, his mother's weakness.

He regarded her again, that unfathomable feeling blooming through him. He couldn't yet put a name to his emotions, maybe they would always defy definition. But he began to recognize the odd sensation the feelings provoked, a worrisome combination of relief and annoyance. It was at once aggravating and soothing to be known by her, to have revealed what he had so long tried to keep hidden. Absolutely no one knew the truth of his parents, not even Ben, who had become like a brother to him in so many ways. But Juniper knew and, what was more, didn't think less of him because of it. The only explanation he could find for that was her youth and inexperience. Too long sheltered by her eccentric family, she hadn't seen or known enough of the world to understand how much his upbringing had set him apart from others.

"I will never be like other men," he informed her.

"Why would you want to be?" she countered.

He scowled. "You worry me, Juni, you really do."

Contrary to everything rational, she beamed. "Now that's the first sensible thing you've said in an age."

Smiling a little in spite of himself, he picked up the machete and faced forward. "Come on, pest. And next time I swing a machete at you, jump out of the way."

"It's cute how you think telling me what to do is less dangerous than a machete," she said. Her expression turned ponderous. "Although I was taught to respect my elders. This is a conundrum."

"I'll elder you," he said and, barely breaking stride, tossed her over his shoulder and continued on his way, smiling when she giggled in delight.

*

John could have walked through the night. He had made his body a tool, a weapon, a trained machine that only occasionally needed fuel. It slept when he told it to sleep and ate when he told it to eat. But Juniper, hale and hardy though she was, was still a normal girl who needed sleep and food.

"Let's rest here," he said, reaching into his pack for water and food. She took a few sips and handed the canteen to him, smiling as she inspected the MRE he gave her.

"I've never had one before. Are they good?"

"Would they replace your Mama's cooking? No. Are they passable enough to be edible? Also no. But they're all we've got," he said. John hated army food, a secret he'd never admit to anyone. But he'd grown up at the feet of two amazing southern cooks, first his mother and then Juniper's mother, both of whom had spoiled him with their talents. Subsisting on the army's diet of bland cafeteria food and MREs the last decade and a half was more of a trial for him than anything else had been.

Juniper laughed and tore open her packet, giving it a sniff. "It doesn't seem so bad," she said.

He could argue with her, tell her it wasn't bad the first time but after the fortieth day in a row it felt almost unbearable. But instead he remained silent, observing her with a smile. It wasn't his way to complain and bellyache about things, but it was more than that. Juniper had a sense of adventure he found endearing. Most women in her position—beaten half-senseless by a gang of rogues who'd kidnapped her, on a forced march through the jungle—would be exhausted at the least, grumpy and overwhelmed at worst. But Juniper had found her inner sparkle, and he realized in that moment it wasn't because youth was on her side; it was just Juniper. She embraced life, had no fear of living in a yurt in the wilds of Honduras, didn't care a whit that she'd been hours without food, water, or rest, and had already resolved herself to move on from the kidnap and assault. If John were looking, Juniper would be exactly the sort of woman he'd go for, all sparkle and sunshine on top, all grit and substance beneath. But he wasn't looking, he reminded himself as he forced his lips to stop smiling, his eyes to stop staring. He wasn't looking at all.

"Where'd you go?" she asked.

He raised his head, staring at her in question.

"Just now, you went all John Caruthers on me, disappeared inside yourself. What are you thinking about?"

When was the last time someone asked him that question? Certainly his men didn't want to know what went on in his mind, probably figured they were better off not knowing. And they were correct. But the Dunbars liked to know the inner workings of a man. John could almost hear Dustin in Juniper's words, could almost see the tilt of his head as he made his inspection. *What's going on in that quiet but powerful brain of yours, John?* Dustin had a way of making people want to be the best version of themselves. He would slip observations and compliments into conversation so you ended up wanting to live up to his words. Under his tutelage, John came to think of himself as someone intelligent, someone who gave thought before action, both things Dustin seemed to value in him.

Juniper waited him out, staring at him with the same considerate intensity her father used to, back in the day. "You're so lucky," he blurted, not what he meant to say at all.

She blinked at him, confused. "Pardon?"

"You're so lucky, Juni, to have a father like yours, a mother like yours, a family like yours. Do you know how lucky you are?"

"I do," she agreed, nodding.

"Do you, though? Do you know how many kids I see come up from basic who have nobody? Who join the army because it's all they can think of to do with their lives?"

"Boys like you were, you mean," she clarified.

He gave a curt nod.

She ate her MRE in thoughtful silence a few beats before she spoke again. "But you always had us, John. We were always there, backing you up, surrounding you, loving you. When you went away, it left a hole in our family."

"For you, maybe." He had always been Juniper's inexplicable favorite. An entire family of loving, delightful people, and she'd chosen the standoffish, recalcitrant teenager as her own.

"No," she shook her head hard. "My parents set a place at the table for you every holiday, hoping you'd come home. They bought you presents that became a pile in the hall closet. Sometimes I'd see them glance at the door, sort of expectant, and I'd know they were looking for you." She paused and shook her food packet. "The same as me. I don't think I ever stopped looking at the door. And then…"

He watched her intently, waiting for her to continue. A shadow passed over her face, and she shuddered. John felt a prickle of alarm, but he quickly dismissed it. Nothing bad could have happened to her, not really, not with her loving family on standby. "And then what?"

She took a breath and pushed the dark mood away, giving him a smile. "And then at some point I suppose I stopped waiting, stopped jumping every time I heard a car in the drive. At some point I guess it sank in and I accepted that you didn't claim us the same way we claimed you."

He finished his meal, chewing each bite the precisely prescribed number of times. When that was finished, he folded the MRE packet and slipped it back in his pack. "It has nothing to do with claiming or not claiming, Juni. It's just how it is. It was time for me to move on, grow up, do other things."

"We loved you. Didn't you love us?"

She looked so much like the little girl she had been then, plaintive and pouting, her pretty face turned up to his in silent supplication. Back then it had been an invitation to pick her up and hold her close. He felt the same urge today and balled his hands into fists, resisting the temptation. "I can't love. You know that."

Her lashes fluttered. "I don't know that. Of course you can. You're a man, the same as every other."

The same as my father, his mind filled in the unspoken rejoinder. "What happened with my parents, all those years ago, it…broke something inside me. Made me unable to connect in that way." He thought she understood, but maybe she was too young back then to realize how it had been, how hard her family tried to love and mend him, how useless and wasted their efforts had been. He remained unable to feel, unable to love, unable to attach.

Juniper watched him a moment in shocked silence, her mouth slightly ajar. He could feel the weight of her judgment as her mind ran the information through its new filter. *So that's why he's like that, why he's always been like that. That's why he behaves the way he does, why he rejected us all.* He could practically hear her thoughts, so it came as something of a surprise when she wadded up her empty food packet and tossed it hard at his face, pelting him between the eyes. Her eyes flashed fire, and she stood up as she yelled, "Nonsense, you forsaken idiot."

CHAPTER 13

J ohn bent and retrieved her discarded wrapper. He uncrumpled it, flattening it before folding it nicely and neatly into thirds. Then he stuffed it into his pack and forced himself to take five deep breaths.

He did not like to be yelled at.

He did not like to be called an idiot.

He did not like having to explain himself to an insubordinate, civilian or otherwise.

And he especially did not like being painfully pelted in the face by a balled up foil wrapper.

"Excuse me?" he said, his silky tone a warning sign of his repressed anger.

"You heard me," she said, hands on hips now. "What kind of fool-hardy notion has taken hold of your senses? And how many times do I have to beat you in the head to get it back out?"

"You don't know what you're talking about," he assured her.

"No, *you* don't know what you're talking about," she argued.

"You're only twenty two," he said, tone dismissive.

She jutted a finger in his face. "So help you if you tell me my age one more time. I may be a decade behind you in age, but I am leaps and bounds ahead of you in people skills and intuition."

That was probably true, and John hated it. He prided himself in being the smartest person in the room, always, but his people skills *were* lacking, his intuition nonexistent. "Juni," he started, but she interrupted.

"Don't you *Juni* me, Bear. I was there, remember? I was there for all of it. Do you know my first memory, the first one in my whole life, is the day you showed up on our doorstep? So big and gruff and silent. And I thought you were an overgrown teddy bear, sent there expressly for me. And I was right because, exasperated as you sometimes were with me, you were nothing but patient and gentle, kind and attentive. Do you think my parents didn't know what they were doing when they paired me with you? Do you think they had some sort of monumental lapse in judgment when they sent their youngest off with the new kid? Or do you think they realized you had a special way with me, that in a large family it's easy to get overlooked and sidetracked and..." her voice broke and she took a breath before continuing, "and you never sidetracked me. You always made time for me, always talked to me, cared for me, spent time with me, played with me, taught me."

"First of all I had no choice," he tried, but she interrupted him again.

"Really? Because I don't seem to recall anything else they were able to make you do that you didn't want to."

He blinked in surprise. That part was true. He had been a proud, stubborn teenager and nothing, absolutely nothing, had been able to make him do what he hadn't already intended to do. "But I was a glorified babysitter. Someone had to make sure you didn't die."

"Yes, and that someone was *you*. Face it, John, you were my person. And what's more, I was yours. And if that's not love, what is? So don't sit there and tell me you are incapable of love because I know firsthand it's not true. You can lie to everyone else in your life, you can lie to yourself, but do not lie to me."

She said the last five words loudly and deliberately, as if they were each set off by exclamation points. *Do! Not! Lie! To! Me!* and John had that feeling again, the one he couldn't put a name to. It made him squeamish to be around Juniper now and maybe, *maybe,* the feeling was fear. Maybe John didn't recognize it at first because he wasn't afraid of anything else. But why would he be afraid of Juniper, a slip of a girl he'd known forever?

She remained staring at him, chest puffing in and out, cheeks flushed, dimple flashing dangerously. The strange feelings inside of John turned from a simmer to a rapid boil and he was as fascinated by them as he was leery. Why did he want to haul her close and, at the same time, shove her far away and run? And why did he get the sense that, in their new dynamic, Juniper was the one with all the power? She seemed to know something in this scenario he didn't, as if they were in a play where he hadn't yet received the lines, but she had. And she knew them all by heart. The way she looked at him, the way she studied him when she thought he wasn't looking, it wasn't like she tried to figure him out. It was like she already had him figured out and was instead attempting to find the softest way to break it to him, the news of who he was.

Worse, he had absolutely no idea what to say or do next. The army was his comfort zone. He was in uniform and on the job, but never before had it involved a woman in this way, and certainly never a woman like Juniper.

He could feel all the feelings building inside him, searching for release. As he saw it, he had three options: 1. Yell at her. Tell her where to get off and why. Tell her to stop rooting around in his life, trying to upset the balance. 2. Kiss her. That one was way more shocking and even more intriguing. 3. Regain his lost control, fall back on his good friend, Reason.

He closed his eyes, took a breath, and patted his pocket. When he opened his eyes, Juniper looked at him like maybe he'd lost his mind. He'd come close, too close. But he was much too disciplined to toss in the towel and have an emotional outburst now. "If you're finished with your food, I brought your toothbrush." He fished in his pack and presented her with her toothbrush and toothpaste.

She glanced from the proffered items, to him, and back to the items again before bursting into loud tears and tossing herself into his embrace with a weepy, *"Oh, Bear."*

He caught her, as was apparently their custom now, and wrapped her in a tight hug, his hand smoothing over her tangled hair. Somehow that action felt less clumsy than it had before, both more practiced and more natural. Perhaps practice was the key to learning how to be around other humans, except he didn't want to practice on anyone. Well, no one besides Juniper, he amended.

"I don't know why you're crying," he said when it seemed like her tears might never end. Was she angry? Hurt? Happy? He had no idea.

"Me neither," she said, laughing a little. She pulled away to regard him and he found himself using his thumbs to wipe her tears, an action he didn't realize he knew how to do. Maybe it was instinct or maybe he had learned long ago how best to soothe her, when she was a child, and some part of him remembered.

"I don't know, Bear. I just don't know."

"What don't you know?" he asked, taken aback by the soft tenderness in his tone. Before these last few days with Juniper, he had no idea his voice could sound like that, had no idea gentleness was a hidden part of his being. And, if he were being honest, he kind of liked it.

"Before, everything was so clear. And now you're here. And I just… don't know." More tears leaked out of her eyes, but he wiped them away before they could make landfall.

"Nothing has changed, Juni."

"Everything has changed, Bear."

He squinted. "How has it changed?"

"Because I found you. Or you found me. Maybe we found each other. I don't know. I just don't know."

"You've had a long, difficult day. You're tired, and now you're getting all worked up over nothing. Lots of people have this sort of delayed reaction to an adrenaline rush."

"You?" she asked, her dimple making a return with the hint of a smile.

"All the time. They call me the weeping major."

She stared at his chest, thinking. "So we're clear, you don't find anything…cosmic…about our sudden reappearance in each other's lives?"

He snugged her slightly closer. "Juni, I don't find anything cosmic in anything. Life happens and then you die."

"Really?" She stared up at him, lashes dewy, pretty face tear-streaked, puffy lips still slightly trembly, and something in his chest kicked hard.

"Really," he said, a choked whisper because, all of a sudden he wasn't certain he believed himself. "Why does it matter to you so much?"

"Because what if I'm making a terrible decision marrying another man when you're my destiny?"

"Whether or not you're making a terrible decision only you can answer, but I am not your destiny, Juniper."

"But how do you know?" she asked.

"Because I don't believe in destiny. I believe in facts and logic, in rational decision making."

"And yet here we sit, two Alabama kids, in the middle of the jungle in Honduras."

"Only one of us is a kid," he reminded her.

"I graduated college," she said, peeved.

"So did I, a decade ago."

"Fine, you're too old for me, too emotionally unavailable for me, too dedicated to your career for me. Now go away. Oh, wait, you can't. Because we're stuck together in the jungle in Honduras."

He grinned, smoothing his hand over her wayward hair. "I shouldn't like it so much when you act like that."

"But you do," she prompted.

"But I do," he agreed. "Everything you said is true, though. I am too old for you, too emotionally unavailable for you, too dedicated to my career for you."

"And what am I too much of for you?" she asked.

"I don't take your meaning," he said. His eyes were drawn to her lips as if magnetized. Every time he thought he had a handle on it, they'd stray there again. He watched them as they spoke, wondering if they were as soft and full as they looked.

"You've got it all figured out why you're wrong for me. Why am I wrong for you? Too emotional? Too immature? You don't like smart girls with glasses?"

"I like your glasses and I love your smarts," he declared, the impassioned statement taking them both by surprise.

"You find me unattractive in other ways?" she prompted. Her dimple sprang to life, giving away her amusement at his expense.

"You know that's not it," he said, exasperated.

"Do I? How do I know? You haven't said one word to suggest otherwise."

"Pretty girls always know they're pretty," he groused.

"Do handsome men always know they're handsome?" she returned, poking him.

"I don't...that's not..." he swiped a mosquito from the back of his neck. "You think I'm handsome?"

"Do you think I'm pretty?"

"Are you going to make me say it? Are you so insecure you need the words that badly?" he asked.

"Absolutely," she said, nodding.

"You're very attractive."

Her nose wrinkled in distaste. "You remember when the Plainfields got that fancy new Buick? My daddy said the same thing about that. *It's a very attractive car.* Is that what you think, John? Am I am Buick to you?"

"Of course not, Juniper," he said, fairly certain he blushed.

Her eyebrows rose. "I don't even rate as high as a Buick? Am I at least a Pinto?"

"You're not a Pinto," he exclaimed.

She gasped in mock affront, pressing her hand to her heart, affecting a wounded expression. "Not even a Pinto?"

"You're beautiful," he bellowed. "Is that what you want to hear? You're so beautiful it hurts to look at you. Even puffy and bruised you're the loveliest thing I've ever seen." His fingers reached out, tentative and gentle, to touch her split lip.

"Well, that was worth the pains it took to get there," she said softly, and now she was the one who blushed, a pleasant flush that only worked to increase her prettiness. It was so potent now he almost groaned with the effort it took not to reach for her. "And for what it's worth, Bear, all those girls were right to have a crush on you. If they could see you now." She shook her head. "Wow, just wow."

He'd never been anybody's "wow" before, nor had he wanted to be. He had never understood the give and take between men and women, never understood the fascination or the draw. Obviously he saw the appeal in sex, but for most of his men the desire to be with a woman went beyond that, and he had judged them as being too soft, too weak to know what was good for them. But now he almost sort of understood. Being with Juniper was a different sort of challenge, a new kind of one upmanship than sparring with an opponent. And somehow he felt the stakes were even higher than life and death.

"We should get some sleep," he whispered, his fingers still making a slow trail around her mouth.

"Really? Shouldn't we be back at camp by now?" she whispered, leaning in to his touch, leaning in to *him*. No one had ever done that before. People usually leaned away.

"We're not going back to camp," he muttered, not paying attention to her reaction at first. Would it be so bad to kiss her? One little kiss, for the sake of their long friendship? It could be a hello kiss, they'd never had one of those. Or a nice-to-see-you-again greeting. That was a thing people did, right?

"What did you say?" she demanded, moving away from his touch.

With effort, he paused and reviewed the conversation in his head. Unable to figure it out, he blundered ahead. "We're not going back to camp. I'm taking you to the base so you can get a flight out."

CHAPTER 14

Anger was a useless emotion. Long ago John came to the conclusion that there was no room for it in the army. Most people thought he was an angry person, but it wasn't true. He was an *impatient* person. He had zero tolerance for weakness, laziness, or stupidity. Not in himself or in others. But anger was something altogether different, a slow-leaking poison that could eat a man from the inside. He'd cut it out of his life from an early age, mostly due to the demands of army life. They lived in close quarters, worked side by side. If something happened that triggered his anger, he worked to let it go as soon as possible. He wondered, as he and Juniper lay in thick silence side by side in his hammock, if she was coming to the same inevitable conclusion. How could you maintain anger at the person who held your life in his hands?

There was only one hammock, a light nylon contraption that could be folded down to a nub and, when unfurled, easily hung between two trees. John didn't mind sleeping on the ground, but the nature of the jungle made that impossible. If the spiders didn't get you, the snakes would. And then there were the jaguars. So now he and Juniper lay pressed into one indistinguishable form, sausage like, while she stewed in her anger and he tried not to do anything to upset her further. At first she'd tried to hold herself stiffly away from him, but it wasn't possible, not with the way her body was forced to curve into his in the hammock. For his own comfort, he'd eased his arm around her. It rested on her back for a bit but then, as if of its own volition, began to make a few gentle circles. With each one, John noticed a bit of tension drain out of her and now each pass felt like a subtle victory until at last her palm unfurled from its clutched fist and curled into his shirt, twisting it into a possessive little ball.

"Why?" she finally asked. "Why are you making me go? Why are you sending me away?"

"To keep you safe," he said, his hand picking up the pace on her back.

"I'm safe with you," she said, and the words did something to him, satisfied some primal part of him he didn't know existed until then.

"Yes, but I'm leading a mission here. I can't be with you every minute."

She tensed again. "I don't need a babysitter."

He backtracked. "Of course you don't. Do you know what's going on here? With the Contras and the Sandinistas?"

"I know the fundamentals."

"Then you know it goes farther than Honduras and Nicaragua. On a grander scale, this is between us and the Soviets. There can be no missteps. It's up to me and me alone to make certain this doesn't spiral into another Bay of Pigs type situation."

"That's a lot of pressure," she said, and now she was the one rubbing a soothing little circle on his stomach.

"It's not the pressure that bothers me, I'm used to it. It's the possible loss of innocent life. These people, the locals, did nothing to spark this skirmish but, as ever, they're caught in the middle. Already impoverished, they're about to lose even more in a battle that has nothing to do with them." He took a breath and told her the absolute truth. "When I heard an American scientist was camping in the jungle, I was annoyed. When I heard it was a woman, I was concerned. But, Juni, when I found out it was you, I lost my head. I've never been in a situation where someone I know is in the crosshairs. I cannot concentrate on what I need to do here if there's even one part of my mind wondering if my actions are putting you in harm's way. I…I didn't handle it well, kidnapping you like that. And I…I'm sorry. But I need you safe, and for that to happen, I need you gone."

She was quiet for a bit, digesting. The silence between them was no longer heavy or tense. Instead it was cozy and comfortable. A rare breeze kicked up, swinging them gently. "So you, maybe, don't want me to go, a little bit?"

He swallowed hard, fighting for time. It wasn't in his nature to lie, but neither was it natural to bare his heart. "I don't know," he said slowly. "This is…different."

He could feel her smile against his chest. "Different's not bad, Bear."

"I don't do different. My life is fairly prescribed."

"Want to know what I think?" she asked.

"Yes," he said after a pause, realizing with some surprise he meant it. He was used to telling his men what to think and how to feel. It came as a slight shock to realize not only was there someone whose life he couldn't order to his satisfaction but he was curious to hear her insight.

"I think you're predictably amazing at this, at being a major in the army."

He waited her out, sensing there was more. He was correct.

"But." She flattened her palm on his chest and tipped her face so she could see him better. "You're only living half a life here, John, cutting yourself off from all emotion, from all contact with people who care about you. Someday your career will be over, and then what?"

Her hair was a mass of sweaty tangles, perceptive eyes too bright as they studied him. Seemingly of its own volition his hand slid to her face and cupped it, his thumb rubbing along the edge of her jaw. Had anything ever been as soft and sweet as Juniper was in his arms? Not that he could remember.

"Juni, the reality is that I likely won't make it to retirement."

"I don't believe that," she said, stubbornly, he thought.

"This assignment, filled with enemy insurgents, heavily armed with Soviet weapons, is a cakewalk compared to some. You have no idea the places I go, the things I do. By all rights I should be dead already."

"But you're not. And to preemptively live like you are or will be is nothing less than cowardice."

Everything within him tightened and stilled. If there was one thing John couldn't stand, it was cowardice, not in himself or in others. For more than half his life he had been training himself to overcome all natural fear, to run toward danger instead of away, to disregard his own life in favor of others. To hear someone accuse him of it now sent rage flooding all the cells of his body. "You have no idea," he ground out, words sparking out of him like bullets. If Juniper had any sense, she would run away and scramble up the nearest tree to escape his wrath. But of course she didn't because, as ever, she didn't fear him like she should. The woman lacked fundamental regard for her own safety, now more than ever.

"Don't I?" she countered, quirking her eyebrow in a way that made him squirm with something that felt a whole lot like fear. To his further dismay, he had to swallow past a large lump of that bile-tasting substance to speak.

"I am not afraid of anything."

She grasped his shirt and used it as an anchor so she could pull herself level with his face, hovering a hairsbreadth away. "Wanna bet?"

She was so close he could feel the wind from her lashes whenever she blinked. Her breath puffed out, moistening his lips with each exhalation. "What are you doing?" he said, his voice an embarrassing rasp.

"Testing a theory," she whispered.

"What's my objective?" he asked, his index finger brushing a soft curl at her temple.

"You'll know it when you see it," she replied, tilting her head so it was the perfect angle to his. And then she hovered, waiting.

He took a deep breath, studying her face from closer up, and then, before she could blink, latched on and flipped her, pinning her beneath him in the close quarters of the hammock.

"First rule of war, Juni. Always make sure you're going to win before issuing a challenge."

There was nowhere for the parts of her body to go but around him. Her arms latched around his neck, one leg curled around his. "Do you think I'm afraid of you?" she asked.

"I think you should be," he replied.

She shook her head, as much as she could in the tight confines "Never. Not once, not for one moment of our lives have I ever been afraid of you, Bear."

"Then what are you, Juniper?" Because he didn't know what she was, nor what she was doing to him. The inability to figure it out, to pin her down and categorize her, was driving him insane.

She studied him in silence as she drew in a long breath, held it, and burst into tears.

"Did I hurt you?" he asked in sudden panic, the return of his soft accent making the words sound even more gentle.

Juniper shook her head and clung tighter, pressing her face to his neck, wetting it with her tears.

"Juni, I must be mashing you. I must have scared you," he argued as he tried to disentangle himself and break away.

"You didn't, I promise. Just…please don't go. Please just hold me," Juniper said, her words barely discernable through desperate weeping.

"Juni," he groaned, feeling as uncertain as he ever had. For him, tears equaled pain. If his past had taught him anything it was that he was always responsible for the pain of those around him.

"Please," Juniper whispered. She sounded so sad, so broken, so un-Juniper. Where was his firecracker? Where was that irrepressible little girl from his memory? What could possibly have happened in her sheltered life to make her this upset? Still, he couldn't deny her request, couldn't deny her anything when she was like this. So he twisted, settling her more comfortably in his embrace. Instead of domineering her, he held her tenderly—cradled, cared for, *protected.*

And it was easier, so much easier, than he'd thought it would be. He even managed to find his voice.

"It's all right. I've got you now. I'm here," he whispered, his hand making whisper-soft passes over her hair. He had no idea it knew how to do such a thing. Some long-dormant instinct must have awakened inside him, telling his body what to do, even though his heart didn't know.

Juniper burrowed against him, exactly as she had as a sleepy toddler. He had forgotten, until this moment, the indelibly soft feel and smell of a sleepy baby. He wasn't certain if the memory was so strong he could smell it now or if Juniper still smelled the same. Eventually his hand gave up its steady movement. As her sobs began to quiet to pitiful sniffles, his fingers wound in her cornsilk hair, tangling in her curls and holding on with a shockingly proprietary grip.

"I'm so tired, Bear. So very tired," Juniper whispered at last.

"Go to sleep, Juni. I've got you," he whispered, his lips moving against the top of her head.

Juniper shuddered, almost as if in relief, slid her arm over his waist like an anchoring tether, and fell asleep.

He stared at the tree canopy overhead for a bit, unable to make heads or tails of anything that had happened since Juniper's sudden reappearance in his life.

He woke as he always did, fully alert and ready for action. The only difference this time was Juniper, still snuggled in his embrace. *We should go,* he thought. But they didn't. He lay perfectly still, letting her warmth seep into him. How long since he'd had physical contact with another human being? Too long. He'd convinced himself it didn't matter, that he was a machine who could live without it, and now that was being revealed for the shallow lie it was. Juniper's little body next to his felt like an icepack on a throbbing bruise, healing in all the ways. But instead of letting the comfort wash over him, he fought it, annoyed that he had to. He was above human needs and emotions. If not, what had it all been about?

He thought Juniper was still asleep until she spoke. "Tell me about your life."

"No," John replied, tone terse and clipped at all the unwelcome feelings now rumbling inside him. Blast her softness for making him feel weak. She tipped her face to his, causing him to tilt his down to hers. And when he saw that he'd wounded her with his words, his heart gave a painful wrench. "Most of it's classified," he added begrudgingly.

Her face softened with a smile. Juniper first thing in the morning was a sight, all wild hair and luscious features—full lips and eyes, long lashes no longer obscured behind her glasses. His finger seemed to have a mind of its own as it reached out and skimmed the feather soft lashes. He finished with one eye and stared at his finger in betrayal. What was his body doing to him? Worse, would he ever be able to get it back under control again?

"Tell me about West Point," she urged, shifting to snuggle impossibly closer, tilting her head so it rested over his heart.

"West Point was the only time in my life I ever felt close to belonging." Even though it was more than he usually blurted or revealed to anyone, he didn't regret it. It eased a little of the ache inside him to be able to tell her things he'd told no one else. And, knowing him and his past, she understood.

"Because they were all soldiers, like you," she said, proving that she did, in fact, understand. Other men joined the army because it was an out, something to do to pass the time until they figured out their real lives. For John and others like him, it had been the entire goal and journey all along. He wasn't a temporary soldier; he was a soldier for life. Every molecule of his body had been poured into his training, into making him the killing machine he now was.

"Yes. We were all driven, focused, determined. I...I had friends, Ben in particular. We still keep in contact, all of us." If there was wonder in his tone, he couldn't seem to help it. Nobody had ever wanted to be his friend, save Juniper and her siblings. He'd been too odd, too inside his own head, too *other*. But at West Point they'd seemingly all been like him, career soldiers who understood without being told that they were laying their lives on the sacrificial altar, giving up their rights to autonomy. The US government owned them now. A few of them had families, and John didn't understand the discrepancy. *No one can serve two masters.* His master was the United States Army. He could have no other.

Juniper squirmed, making him realize he'd been unconsciously squeezing her during his mental aside. He eased his grip and then, as if that force that had taken over his body was still in charge, kissed the top of her head. Then remained staring intently at the canopy overhead. *What on earth is happening to me?*

Juniper, of course, saw nothing amiss in the strange act. For her and her family, affection was so free and easy it wasn't anything they ever had to think about. For John it was monumental, a temporary act of insanity.

"I'd like to meet your friend," Juniper murmured sleepily.

You won't, he wanted to say. But somehow he didn't. There would never be a time when Juniper Dunbar met any of his friends, never be a time when she comingled and immersed herself in his solitary life. He'd given all that up years ago, his right to be like other men. But the moment was so peaceful, so perfect that not even he wanted to mess it up. They lay in cozy silence, John's foot twisting slightly to swing them back and forth.

"I could stay like this forever," Juniper murmured, the words muffled by his chest.

So could I, he thought. The thought was so alarming that, with one swift motion, he flipped himself out of the hammock and landed lightly on his feet. "Time for breakfast."

Juniper remained in the hammock, staring up at him with an amused smile that said she knew exactly what went on in his head and exactly how hard he worked to keep her at bay. He should meet that look head on and stare her down. He should give her another lecture about the isolated nature of his life. Instead he turned tail and ran away, avoiding her steady gaze.

CHAPTER 15

John intended to eat the MRE rations he'd brought, and they did. But Juniper added her own special spin on things, gathering fruit and unknown things from the plants and trees around them.

"Always bring a botanist to a knife fight," she said, dumping her bounty on the ground between them and using his knife—without asking—to peel and cut it.

John tried to ignore her by pretending to read, as if he weren't watching every infinitesimal movement of her fingers as they peeled the fruit, every flit of her expressions as each thought changed them. Juniper was not the kind of person who masked her emotions nor kept them to herself. Her face was an open book, this morning alight with curiosity and adventure. John wanted to roll his eyes. Of *course* she would think traipsing through the Honduran jungle, surrounded by armed militants, was a fun escapade. Of course she wouldn't realize how much danger they were in. It was as if she had been biologically mis-programmed to seek danger in all the worst ways, himself included.

"What are you reading?" she asked, interrupting his rage-fueled monologue. "I see you pat that book in your pocket all the time. Is it the Bible?"

"In a manner of speaking. It's *Meditations*," he replied.

"Marcus Aurelius," she returned, shocking him into such utter speechlessness he could only stare at her, mouth slightly agape. And then she burst into a fit of giggles he could in no way understand. Laughter wasn't usually the response when people referenced Stoic philosophers.

"What?" he snapped, annoyed that his blasted curiosity got the better of him. But her mind was so unfathomable he couldn't possibly guess why she laughed.

"It all makes sense now," she said, wiping tears of amusement.

Absolutely nothing made sense, at least to John. "How so," he pressed, annoyed that she made him draw it out of her.

"My dad made me do my senior thesis on that book." She giggled again and pressed her palm to her mouth, trying to push it back in. "Oh, Dad."

"Why does that make you laugh?" he asked. "It's a great book." It was the perfect book, the one on which he'd built the entire foundation of his life. His Uncle Bailey gave it to him as a high school graduation present. To John it had read like a life manual, teaching him how to deal with his pesky emotions, once and for all.

"It's a very good book, but it was so random. But of course it wasn't random at all. It was because of you." Still smiling, she shook her head.

"You're going to have to dumb it down for me here, Juni. What does your high school thesis have to do with me?"

She paused mid-mango and regarded him. "Everything, Bear. Everything has everything to do with you. Why else do you think my dad made me read that book, if not for you?"

"But why would he make you read it for me?" he asked. It was as if she spoke in riddles.

"It's what I've been telling you," she said.

"Juni, I haven't understood a word that's come out of your mouth since I stepped into your tent," he replied.

Laughing, she set aside the fruit and faced him. "I adored you. Always. From the moment I saw you until the moment you left and every moment after. You were my hero, my ideal. My sneaky dad knew and used it against me, assigning me a book he must have known you were reading."

"Bailey probably told him," John mused. She resumed slicing fruit, but his gaze didn't waver from her profile. "Why, Juni? Why waste all that time adoring a guy like me? Surely there must have been other people in your life, other boys more worthy of your attention."

"There were other people. No one more worthy," she said.

John huffed a sigh of frustration. "What is it with you Dunbars and your inability to see people as they are?"

"Maybe we see the potential," she said, holding out his knife with a piece of fruit on the tip.

"Certifiable, the lot of you," he said, but he took the fruit and downed it. "What else did your dad have you read?"

"The usual: Plato, Dante, Shakespeare," she said, shrugging.

"By now you must have realized there was nothing usual about it," he said.

She grinned and edged closer, plopping down beside him. "Obviously I meant the usual for the Dunbars."

"I have to say I received a far superior education with your folks than I would have in public school," he said. "Unconventional though it was."

Juniper wrapped her arms around her knees, staring dreamily into the distance. "I'm going to do the same with my kids. I'm going to teach them myself, and I'm going to teach them all the most important things, the things we were taught."

"What about your big time botany degree?" he asked, nudging her.

"Who says they're incompatible?" she asked, nudging him in return. "I'll bring them along on jobsites for some real world experience."

"You're going to have it all, huh?" he asked.

"Every last bit," she said. She opened her arms and spread them wide. "I'm going to wring every drop of living from life, Bear."

"And this guy you're going to marry, he's okay with all this? Home-schooling your kids, giving them a classical education?"

"He'll have to be, won't he? No compromise, not when it comes to my children."

"Maybe I should write him a warning letter, inform him what he's in for," he said.

"If he doesn't know by now, it's too late for him," she said.

"I suppose he got the idea the first time he met your people. There's nothing quite like the full Dunbar effect," he said.

"You survived it," she said.

"Barely," he said, smiling when she rolled her eyes. Not for the first time he had the uncomfortable realization that he owed her family more than he could currently repay. He may not have fit the Dunbar mold—affectionate, easy with his words and emotions—but he had received six years of solid education and financial support. That counted for something; in fact it counted for everything. He shuddered to think where he might have ended up, if not for them and his Uncle Bailey. With the baggage he'd been hauling, it was likely he would have turned to a life of crime. Instead he was given a first rate education, one that propelled him to the top of his class at West Point, no easy feat for a group of determined and ambitious soldiers.

"I don't know about this boy of yours, Juni. What kind of man lets his fiancée go off to the jungles of Honduras?"

"It's cute how you think he let me," she replied.

"What about your parents? Free spirited as they are, I also know they're cognizant of world events. Surely they must have had some reservations about this little venture, given the current climate."

"My parents have always wanted me to follow my dreams, no matter where they might lead."

He had no argument for that because it was probably true. The Dunbars were good about that sort of thing, about enabling their children to follow their respective passions. With sudden clarity he remembered the day he told her father he wanted to go to West Point. *Sounds like a fine tradition to carry on, John. I'm sure your Uncle Bailey will be proud. You'll make an amazing soldier, one I'll be proud to say I know.*

John hadn't responded with more than a nod, but those words had made a little buzz of warm pride in his midsection. Even though Dustin Dunbar hadn't been his father, his opinion had meant a tremendous amount to John. He hadn't agreed with his warm and fuzzy methods, but he'd realized the older man was wise and good, two things his own father had never been.

He realized Juniper stared at him and probably had been for some time. "What?" Of course it wasn't possible that she could read his sentimental thoughts, but he felt embarrassed over them regardless. Sentimentality was one of the soft and useless emotions he thought he'd weeded out long ago. And now it was once again rearing its ugly head. He began to see the appeal of scourges. If he had one now, he'd flail himself into compliance.

"No one is as still as you, as silent. I thought I'd imagined it, the way you become like a statue. But it's even more pronounced than in my memory. You must be terrifying to anyone insane enough to go against you."

Of course Juniper always said the thing he expected least. She was all warm softness. She should hate the cold, dead parts of him. Instead her tone rang with approval.

"I've killed more men than you could imagine. Hordes of them, sometimes with a gun or knife. But mostly with my hands." He held his hands up for her inspection. By all rights they should be dripping with blood.

"You're a soldier," she said.

Once again her words had the opposite effect. They should have eased him, but they didn't. "It's not that simple," he said.

"Simplify it for me," she commanded.

He took a breath and held it as he tried to figure out how best to proceed. "A lot of men are soldiers. None of the others are like me."

"You mean they're not as good as you," she said.

"It's not about good or bad. It's about," he made a fist and thumped it over his heart.

She blinked at him, for the first time looking disturbed. He should be relieved that she was finally starting to understand, but instead he felt disappointed and apprehensive. At long last she would see the truth of what he did, of who he was. And her opinion of him would change. It should. It needed to. It was beyond time for her to grow up and get over the fantasy she'd held that he was some kind of hero. But now, faced with the imminent prospect, he suddenly wanted to go back, to be the kind of man she looked up to.

"You must be joking," she said.

He shook his head.

She huffed an annoyed little puff.

While he was on this path, he might as well get it all out in the open. He took another breath and made himself say the words. "The shrinks say I'm a sociopath."

She did the shocked blink thing again and then, in true Juniper fashion, let out a burble of laughter that sounded like pure delight. "Stop it." She gave his arm a little shove.

"Once again I do not understand your laughter," he informed her.

"You are not a sociopath. My lands. Who are they letting be psychologists these days? Idiots. Morons, all of them." She dabbed at her wet eyes and snorted another laugh.

"Juniper, they're not wrong," he exclaimed, scowling.

She set her hands on her hips and tried to mimic his stern expression, "Bear, yes they are."

"Woman, you're on my last nerve. I am telling you there is something fundamentally wrong with me and you're laughing about it."

"Because there may be a few things wrong with you, but a lack of conscience isn't one of them," she said.

"You have no idea. *No idea*," he said. His hand waved in her general direction. "Girl, you frustrate me."

She laughed harder. "And that, you daft boy, is exactly why you're not a sociopath. Do you think I would annoy a sociopath?"

"I think you would annoy Mother Theresa. You could annoy the paint off the side of a barn. You're so annoying, mosquitoes fly away from you in search of less aggravating blood. You're so annoying…"

He never got to finish his list because she pounced, knocking him to the ground. "Ha, pinned ya!"

"I let ya, you infernal brat. I swear, Juniper."

She wove her fingers through his, pressing his palms into the soft flora beneath him. "What do you swear, Major Caruthers? That you are so woefully complex?" She leaned closer. "Shut down?" She leaned closer, bringing her face into sharp relief with his. Her voice dropped to a whisper. "Dangerous?"

"Yes." His voice remained even but he swallowed hard, Adam's apple bobbing pathetically.

"John."

"What?"

"I have a secret."

"What?"

"I'm the one who's dangerous, and you're nothing but a big ball of fluff," she whispered.

"Juniper, be serious," he said, a tall order since she barely knew how.

"I'm serious as a heart attack. You, Mr. Big and Mighty Major, are lacking key knowledge regarding our current scenario."

"And what knowledge might that be, Miss Dunbar?"

She edged impossibly closer, lips almost brushing his. "Baby, that's for me to know. And you to find out."

One of his hands shook free and cupped her jaw. "You think you're pretty cute, don't you?"

She shrugged one shoulder.

"It so happens you're correct," he said, thumb smoothing along her lip. "You're pretty cute."

"For a kid, you mean," she said.

"I'm not old," he said.

"Prove it," she replied and wagged her brows.

He laughed, a rusty ill-used sound that was probably more terrifying than pleasant. "I swear your parents did not spank you enough."

"They didn't spank me at all," she reminded him.

"It shows. Now back to the other thing." He wrapped both arms around her, ratcheting her up so they were eye to eye, body to body.

"You're very cute, as you know, clever and charming and tempting in all the ways. But you are off limits in every possible way."

"Because you're so old?" she guessed.

"No, you insufferable little runt."

"Because I'm engaged to another man?"

"No, but it's good to hear you remember that little fact when you're flouncing yourself at me," he said.

"Because you…" she tried again, but he pressed his thumb to her mouth, shushing her.

"Why don't you stop tossing out reasons and let me tell you? You are off limits because of me. Because I'm a soldier, always a soldier, only a soldier. And that's never going to change, not for you, not for anybody. I don't know how many times or in how many ways I can say it until you understand."

"I'll never understand because it's not possible that a man such as you, with so much to give, would live half a life because he's too afraid to live the other."

"Juniper." He wriggled from beneath her and sat up, putting his hand to his head. "You don't understand. You couldn't possibly."

"Then explain it to me again," she said, sitting up beside him, criss-cross applesauce.

"I know the safe, sheltered world you sprang from," he said, making the statement an accusation.

"Yes, it's the same place you sprang from," she reminded him.

"But it's not, Juni. It's *not*. I was already broken beyond repair by the time I reached you. Do you not get that? I feel like the man standing on deck of the *Titanic,* warning of the iceberg. And instead of heeding that warning you're gearing up to jump overboard and swim toward it."

"No, that's not what you are. You're the captain who feels like he has to go down with the ship, who drowns needlessly out of misplaced duty."

He shook his head.

She sat up on her knees and gripped his biceps. "Listen to me. You feel like your father ruined you because of what he did. But I happen to know what *my* father did, and that's in there, too. Those six years of being fathered by Dustin Dunbar were not a waste, John. They're part of you, too."

"Maybe, but which part? The bigger part, the part that can kill and destroy without remorse, that's the part that always wins."

"*No.* Don't say that because I know it's not true. If not me, then find someone else, some other super human woman to love and care for."

His hand reached up and caressed her face. Funny how easy that action was becoming for him. "Don't you get it, Juni? If not you, then who? If I can't make it work with someone I've known and cared for forever, someone who knows the truth of why I am the way I am, then what hope do I have with anyone else? I can't, nor do I want to."

She licked her lips and crawled closer, bringing them chest-to-chest, face to face. "Then make it work with me."

"And what about that other boy, that fiancé?" he asked.

"He's not you," she said simply.

He placed a solemn kiss on her forehead. "No."

She frowned, a Juniper expression of outrage that made him smile. "How am I going to change your mind?" she muttered to herself.

"You're not," he answered, even though the question hadn't been directed to him. "Give up. Go back to the boy or find someone else." Even as he said the words they left a sickly taste in his mouth. But better to have her taken care of than pining alone forever. Juniper alone and unloved was unthinkable. Unlike him she was made for the give and take of a romantic relationship.

"You must have forgotten everything if you believe that's going to happen. I won't stop until I change your mind."

"And *you* must have forgotten everything if you believe I ever change my mind, once it's made up. This is my life. I decided long ago, long before I ever entered the army, that it would be a solitary one. I won't inflict myself on someone else the way my father did."

"You are *not* your father. Are you forgetting you had a mother too? What about her part in all this? By all accounts she was wonderful, loving and affectionate."

"And weak. So weak for letting him do what he did to her," he said. Even after all these years he could feel the visceral bitterness and resentment. "If she hadn't loved him like she did, we could have moved on. She might still be alive."

"You think love is what killed her?" she asked.

"I know it," he answered, tone harsh.

"Did you also consider that the same love you try to disparage is what saved your life that night? Despite being terrorized by your father, your mother made her way to you and put you out of that house. It was love that gave her the courage to do that. Why do you only see the weakness of the emotion and not the bravery?"

He opened his mouth to answer and found that he couldn't because she was right—he had never once thought of it that way. He knew his mother loved him, of course. She had always showered him with love, always took good care of him, shielded him, protected him. But he had spent so much of his life resenting her for capitulating to his father that he never once stopped to realize how much courage she also possessed. During the rare times his father turned his wrath on John, it had been his mother to intervene and put a halt to it, despite knowing she would then take the beating herself. *My mother was some kind of soldier,* he thought, the realization so startling he almost toppled over.

Juniper, pressing her advantage when she had him on the ropes, continued her advance. "Our lives are more than one thing, Bear. They're a tapestry. Your father is a part of that tapestry, but so is my father. So is your mother. So is my mother. And so am I. You and I, we are connected by too many threads to pull asunder." She wove her fingers together, holding them up as demonstration.

John was confused, and he didn't like it. Confusion and uncertainty made him angry. "This was all settled long ago, long before you came back around," he huffed.

Juniper beamed and grasped his shirtfront, giving it a tug. She knew she was knocking him off kilter, drat her and her ways. "All I'm saying is think about it a bit. Because I think you and I could make some beautiful babies, Major Caruthers."

His jaw dropped and his cheeks flushed. "Juniper Dunbar. I ought to wash your mouth out with soap. My lands, putting those thoughts out there. It's indecent. And you're too young."

"Did I offend the innocent Major's sensibilities?" she mused. "Apparently the army has only prepared you for killing, but not for loving."

"That's exactly what I've been trying to tell you," he said, exasperated.

"No, I do not, and I will not accept it. There is more to you than soldiering. I'm going to make you see. This is my solemn vow."

"Your solemn vow is a fruitless fool's pursuit," he said.

"Odd, that's what I said about *your* solemn vow," she returned.

"What did I used to do to shut you up, back in the day? I can't remember," he said.

"A sucker usually worked," she reminded him.

"I'm fresh out," he said.

"Guess you'll have to find something else then," she said, tipping her face toward his.

He was tempted, so tempted to give in and kiss her. But for both their sakes he couldn't. He hadn't spent the past decade maintaining perfect control over himself, only to lose it now when it counted most. She could easily kiss him, but she wouldn't. They both knew he would have to be the one to break first. And he wouldn't, couldn't. He shook his head slowly back and forth.

Juniper emitted a puff of annoyance but soon found her smile. "We still have plenty of time left."

"You underestimate my self-control."

"You underestimate my determination," she returned.

"You always have to have the last word."

"You do remember." She chucked him under the chin, stood, and put down a hand to help him up. He folded the hammock, packed his bag, and they set off through the jungle, hand in hand once again.

CHAPTER 16

They walked for a long time, their progress slow. John had to cut a careful path with his machete, but that wasn't the reason for their snail's pace. It was because he didn't want to let her go. He would have to hand her off at the base, he knew that and he'd made his peace with it. But he had no idea when he would see her again, or if he ever would. For the first time in his entire career, he was being selfish, plodding when he could have hastened, dreading the moment when he would have to say goodbye.

For her part, Juniper was pleasant company. He had no idea why that should shock him so, but it did. He supposed because he had so little contact with women that he had come to think of them as hysterical, irrational, always requiring more of a man than they were willing to give. Why he should believe any of those things, he had no idea. The women he'd known—his mother, Juniper's mother, and all of Juniper's sisters—hadn't been so. Perhaps it was a defense mechanism to keep himself from wanting things he would never have. It had been easy to tell himself he was better off without a woman because women were too much trouble. But, as ever, Juniper dispelled any of those notions. She was pleasant without being cloying, sunny without being saccharine, highly intelligent and, perhaps most shocking of all, completely rational. There wasn't one topic John broached that she couldn't discuss in depth and with well-reasoned responses. In fact if it was anyone but him talking he might say being with her was the most fun he'd had in recent memory, or possibly ever.

Since his days with the Dunbars, John had enjoyed a good debate. He'd honed the ability to delve into deep issues without getting emotionally involved. He and Ben had both been on the Dean's Team, West Point's equivalent of debate. But there was something extra special about arguing for sport with a pretty woman, one whose eyes sparked every time she thought of a new angle. He could probably continue this day on repeat for the rest of his life and die happy. But of course he wouldn't, both because he had a job to do and because the day was a blip. Away from the pressures of real life, of course he and Juniper would have fun and get along. But the pressures always came back around, and then what?

Each time he tried to picture the future, he instead conjured the past, the look of panic that would come over his mother's face when his father was in one of his moods. His father's powerful hands as he reached for her throat. The bruises and breaks that lingered long after his father went back on the road, a constant reminder of what would happen again when he returned. How could he willingly subject a woman to that? Least of all Juni, she who was surrounded by such love and care and always had been. Of course she wouldn't, couldn't understand what it was like to be untethered, to have no anchors in the world, holding you accountable. John was a free agent, in all the worst possible ways. It was only because of the army and his great discipline that he kept himself in check. Juniper had her family, would always have her family. They were not the same and never would be, no matter how hard she tried to make it so.

It was late afternoon when he felt the first flicker of unease. Even though he eschewed any type of otherworldly perception, he believed strongly in whatever sixth sense soldiers possessed. Somehow they always seemed to know when trouble was about to begin. John had the feeling now. He held up his hand for Juniper who, to her credit, immediately went silent and still.

They remained that way—frozen, at one with nature—until John began to distinguish what had triggered his internal alarm. There were people up ahead and to the northeast. He couldn't see them yet, of course, not with the dense jungle vegetation. But he could sense them, could even smell them. They'd recently eaten a meal, one cooked over a fire. The scent of something savory wafted in the air. He recognized the smell and his heart froze before taking a dive. *Cabbage.* Nicaraguans didn't eat cabbage. But the Soviets did.

He pointed to a tree and up. Juniper gave him a nod and turned. He hailed her back and gave her a knife, for snakes not people. In this part of the world they were usually a bigger threat. And since he planned to take care of the people, she'd have to take care of any snakes. She gave him a smile, kissed her finger, and touched it to his cheek. He watched her walk away and shimmy up the tree. Satisfied she was out of harm's way, he faced the camp, stretching his neck back and forth as he walked. He'd sustained a multitude of injuries over his career. Neck strain had to be among the worst.

When he reached the edge of the camp, he paused, silent and still as he made his inspection. There were a few Nicaraguans. These didn't worry him. They were young, hungry, and untrained. *Collateral damage.* The Soviets were the real danger. Not only were they well fed and well trained, but they could also be hopped up on amphetamines, their secret, not-so-secret weapon. Among American soldiers who'd dealt with them in hand-to-hand combat, the stories were legendary, whispers of superhuman strength, the ability to go days without food or sleep. The Eastern Bloc tried to portray their soldiers as so good they were above every human foible. John knew better. They were so drugged their bodies were running on pure adrenaline. John also knew they usually only used the drugs for battle, when they were about to face an enemy. He hoped the element of surprise would give him the advantage, that none of them would have time to dope. Otherwise, he could find himself in trouble.

He made a final count. Not that it mattered how many there were, at least to him. But he liked to check off the numbers in his head. As men began to drop out of the picture, those who remained gave way to fear. Fear was a powerful weapon, perhaps the most powerful weapon. That was why John was glad he'd never felt it. What did he have to fear? Pain? He'd already endured imaginable pain and survived. That he wouldn't return home to his family? He had no family.

Quickly, his eyes flicked to the tree where Juniper now hid. He supposed he had family, or something like it. But Juniper understood the soldier part of him. If he didn't survive, she'd know he'd done his best. And really, that was what it came down to at this moment—keeping Juniper safe. There was nothing, absolutely nothing he wouldn't do in order to succeed in this, his most important mission.

That was his last thought before he turned off his brain and let his body do what he'd trained it to do.

*J*uniper shouldn't watch what was about to happen. She knew John wouldn't want her to. Then again, when had she ever let John's opinion determine her actions?

As she tucked the knife between her teeth and scrambled up the tree, she had the realization that it was John who'd taught her how to climb, a handy skill for a botanist who studied trees. It was also John who taught her proper knife safety. He'd been like her walking, talking personalized scout leader. She had eaten it up, every bit of it. Not necessarily because she was interested in the things he deigned to teach her, but because she was interested in him. Adoration hadn't been nearly strong enough to describe her attachment to him. If she was awake, she was with John. The beauty of homeschool was that he never had to leave her side. And *that* was how Juniper knew John would never hurt her. Because if he had been inclined to do so, he could have on any number of occasions in their youth. He had been exasperated with her, annoyed by the badgering constancy of her presence. But he had never been cruel, never lost his patience or the protective instinct that seemed to be the foundation of their relationship, at least on his behalf.

Her father once told her that Juniper gave John a purpose when he needed one most. *Keep the baby alive,* had been a big responsibility for one so young, but he was the type of kid who had been born ready and responsible. If the rest of her family found the youngest holy terror exhausting, John had found her challenging. Her father knew and understood, almost from the first moment, that John was the sort of person who required a challenge in order to thrive.

Maybe that's what I should do, Juniper thought as she found an appropriate branch and settled in. *Maybe I should make myself a challenge to him, one that needs to be conquered.* How, though? How could she be anything but transparent in her blatant and continued adoration of him?

From her high vantage point, she could see the entire enemy base camp. There appeared to be eight men. Three had the dark complexion and hair of the locals, or possibly neighboring Nicaraguans. Five had the pasty complexion of Soviets. Juniper had encountered a few Soviets in South America and, though she knew they were technically enemies and she wasn't supposed to like them, she couldn't seem to help herself. They had a natural affinity for literature, poetry, and music, all things Juniper loved. More than a few of them had paid her a visit, book in hand and ready to discuss. Her father's liberal love of both people and education had rubbed off on her and she wasn't sorry, even if Bear wouldn't approve.

She couldn't see John, but she knew he was there, waiting and watching. Once he made his move, she should definitely look away, because surely carnage would entail.

When he finally stepped into the clearing, it was like watching a panther stalk its prey and Juniper couldn't look away. Her eyes remained riveted to the scene below her, John stalking to the first man and grasping his head. At the last minute, Juniper squeezed her eyes closed. When she dared open them again, two of the Soviets were down and a third had been alerted.

After that, everything became a blur. That is to say John became a blur. Juniper had no idea how it was possible to move so quickly and with so much precision. She didn't, couldn't look away because it wasn't like watching humans. It was like watching a self-propelled chess match. There was nothing random or uncoordinated about the engagement between John and the remaining two Soviets, who had wised up enough to tag team him now. While the Nicaraguans were busy gathering, loading, and checking their clunky guns, John and the Soviets hashed it out the old fashioned way—with their hands.

When her brothers were younger, they'd loved the old Bruce Lee movies. Watching the three soldiers engage was a bit like that, a series of flips, hits, and jabs that looked so well rehearsed it was hard to believe a stunt coordinator hadn't choreographed them. At one point, when it looked like the Russians would win, Juniper pressed her palm to her mouth, holding back a scream. They had him pinned. One was working his kidneys while the other choked him. And then, inexplicably, they were both down and John was the only one standing, minus the Nicaraguans who all three held their guns on him, weapons shaking.

He said something. Juniper had no idea what. But whatever it was made the three men turn and run away, guns dragging behind them like drooping tails.

She watched as John made a slow sweep of the camp, making certain there were no others. Then he turned, shaded his eyes, and stared up at her tree.

CHAPTER 17

Her arms refused to unclasp from the tree. She hadn't been afraid when she shimmied up, no matter how high she'd had to go to get a good view. She hadn't been afraid while watching John fight all the men, not really. Perhaps she'd had some nibbles of anxiety, but not real fear. Now, however, her body remained welded to the tree, unable to let go in her delayed reaction to the scene she'd witnessed. John could have *died*.

"Juni." John stood at the base of her tree and whispered, staring up at her. Not that he could see her through the thick foliage, but he made a good approximation of where he thought she was. When she made no sound in reply, he whistled for her, the long-forgotten whistle that used to be their signal. She opened her mouth to yell down, but no sound came out.

Approximately four seconds later, he stood beside her in the tree, one arm latched around the trunk. "Didn't you hear me?" he asked.

She nodded.

"Why didn't you answer?"

She blinked.

"You stuck?" he guessed.

She nodded.

Instead of scolding her, or even carrying her, as she thought he might, he surprised her by perching beside her on the big, sturdy branch. For a few moments they sat in silence. His gaze followed hers, over the clearing now strewn with bodies, bodies he'd conquered and discarded.

"You saw everything," he said.

She nodded.

Silence.

"This is what I do," he said at last, quietly, resolutely.

She faced him then. "You think I'm upset?"

"You're hugging this tree like it's your new best friend," he noted.

"A guanacaste," she said.

"What?"

"This tree." She patted its bark. "A guanacaste."

"I thought it was called an elephant ear tree," he said.

"It is." She let out a breath. "I'm not upset."

"Your grip on the guanacaste tree says otherwise," he said.

"I'm not upset with *you*. This is your job. I don't know how many ways to tell you I understand and accept that," she said.

"If you're not upset, then why won't you come down?" he asked.

"Because I was embarrassed," she said.

"What? Why?"

"Because I was afraid. I know you don't like that particular weakness or emotion. I was trying to work through it, and I probably would have, but you got back here too fast. You're so quick, Bear." She tossed him a scowl.

He slid his arm around her and rested his head on hers. "Ah, Juni. Ya vex me, girl."

Her head tilted to land against his shoulder and she snuggled, as much as she could on a high branch. "I know. But how in particular at this moment?"

"I don't like fear in myself, in my men. You're not subject to that particular rule," he said.

"I want to be brave like you," she said. "I've always wanted to be brave like you. It was my biggest life goal as a kid, and I'm afraid I've failed."

"You're brave in other ways," he said.

"What ways?"

"You're not afraid to take a chance on people, to put yourself out there and be vulnerable. That's brave, and that's not me."

"You're so tender," she said, nestling as close as she dared without knocking them off.

He laughed. The sound was so rusty and ill-used he should probably stop doing it. But he couldn't help it; Juniper made him laugh. "How can you say that, after what you just saw?"

"Because you did all that and then scurried up a tree to comfort me. How could I say anything else?" She peeled her head back to regard him.

His heart thundered. He told himself it was the post-fight adrenaline rush, but he didn't believe it. It was her. Juniper Dunbar had this effect on him. Absolutely no one else in his life could make him climb a tree to offer a gentle word, and especially not so soon after a fight that nearly ended in a loss. Usually he withdrew into himself to critique his strategy, to flagellate himself for his mistakes so he could plan better for next time. Now he sat at the top of a tall tree, letting a rare cool breeze blow over him as he shared the space with a pretty girl.

"You know what this reminds me of?" he asked.

"Home?" she guessed.

When he left at eighteen, John cut that word out of his vocabulary. The army was his home, his forever home now. But sitting there with Juniper while the sun sank lower through the trees, it felt the same as it had all those many nights so long ago when, despite his pain and anguish, he knew he would eventually leave the woods and return to the Dunbars for supper. And at that supper he would sit silently while alternating Dunbars tried to outdo each other with talking. Dustin would ask probing questions. The kids would rush to answer. Juniper would scoot her chair as close as possible to his, darting him looks throughout the meal, trying to read his mood and guess his thoughts.

Juniper's mother would eat bites of her meal like a jack in the box, darting up and down to serve her family food. John could picture it, could hear the utter chaos of it, could almost smell it. "Yes, home."

Juniper's hand slid to his thigh and gave it a pat, one that said she knew every thought he'd had before he uttered the hard-won admission. He'd had a home once, filled with people who loved him. As much as he'd tried hard to pretend it didn't exist, it did. Evidence of it was right beside him in this tree.

"Will we make it to the base tonight?" she asked.

"We could, if we pushed it."

"If we don't push it, what happens?"

"We'll spend another night together in the hammock. But I'm almost out of rations. I only packed enough for one day."

"There are much worse things than going hungry," Juniper said.

"Yes," John agreed. He picked up her hand and gave it a squeeze, keeping it tucked in his grasp as they sat still and watched the sun sink deeper in the trees.

❦

*E*ventually they descended the tree. Skirting the insurgents' campsite, they walked a while farther, until it was too dark to see, then set up their own small camp and hammock.

They tucked into the hammock and faced each other, one hand pillowed under their cheeks. His free hand rested on her waist while her free hand reached up to touch the ever-increasing stubble on his cheek.

"Look what happens to you away from the influence of a razor. Your nickname is becoming more appropriate by the moment."

"I'm going to start acting like a bear, too. It's itchy."

Her palm rasped over his cheek and, catlike, he leaned in to her touch. "Tell me about what happened after I went away," he said.

She froze. "What do you mean?"

"With you. You finished growing up. Were there boys?"

"A few," she said.

"Anyone special?"

She tapped his chest.

"Come on, now. Don't fib," he commanded.

"Let me tell you how it went. I wanted to go to prom, rather desperately."

"But you didn't go to school," he interrupted.

"Now you see my problem. So Mama put out the word around town that I was looking for a willing taker."

"Oh, boy." Knowing their town the way he did, he could imagine how that went over.

"Exactly. I had no less than four boys ask me. I, of course, chose the cream of the crop."

"And who might that have been?" he asked, trying to kill that odd stab of what felt a lot like jealousy.

"Del Bradford."

"The bow-legged boy with the braces and buck teeth?"

"He lost the braces and grew into those teeth quite nicely, thank you very much."

"Huh. So how was prom with old Del?"

"It was…ordinary," she said.

"What's wrong with ordinary?" he asked.

"Nothing, if that's what you expect. But I expected spectacular, like all those books I used to read. Instead it was a stinky gym filled with nervous, sweaty teenagers, swaying off beat to outdated tunes."

"Not a love match with Del?"

"One slobbery kiss and I slugged him in the stomach when he tried for more."

"That's my girl," he said. "I bet his mama made you a milkshake." The Bradfords owned the largest dairy farm in the area and saw themselves as promoters of a milk-maximum lifestyle. There wasn't a child in town who hadn't been plied with one or more of Mrs. Bradford's milkshakes. They were so ubiquitous she gave out miniaturized versions for Halloween.

"Chocolate malt," she said cheerfully.

"I could have guessed you were a malt kind of girl. All the extras for Juni."

"It almost made up for the horrid evening. Almost."

"So, was that it? One lousy date with Del?"

"Look who's suddenly curious about my love life," she said.

"I guess I'm curious about a lot of things. More than I realized," he said. "For instance your family," he began, but she preempted him.

"While I'm thinking of it, can I ask you a question and get an honest answer?"

"I'm always honest, Juni. You know that."

"I used to," she said. As a kid, John always told the absolute truth, no matter how painful for him or the hearer.

"That hasn't changed. Nothing has changed. I'm the same then as I am now, only more so. Ask your question, Miss Dunbar."

"A few weeks ago, before you walked into my tent, did you ever imagine it could be this way with a woman? All this touching. So comfortable and easy?"

The question made him squirm, poked the soft spot in his center. But, as he'd said, he would be nothing less than honest when he answered. "No, I never would have guessed. But it's probably because it's you. There's a history there, a foundation and trust."

"Let me ask you another question," she said.

"Ugh, woman," he sighed, somehow knowing the first question would be easier by far.

"If you've come this far in a matter of days with me, can you imagine where we could be in a few years?" she said.

He had absolutely no reply to that. But he also had the sense she'd meant to leave him speechless and pondering. He wanted to find an answer, if only so she didn't win. But he couldn't because he had none.

She leaned closer and kissed his cheek, the brush of her lips unbearably pleasant and soft. "Night, Bear. Sweet dreams."

If he had any dreams, he was certain they'd all be about her. He squeezed his eyes closed and tried not to move, think, or even breathe. His last thought before he dropped to sleep was the same as it usually was lately. *Blast you, Juniper Dunbar.*

CHAPTER 18

By the next morning he'd regained his equilibrium and felt determined not to let Juniper get to him again. He squatted at the edge of the campsite, downing his portion of the remaining MRE in suspicious silence.

"Why you looking at me like that?" she asked, popping a piece of mango she'd located and cut for them.

"Like what?" he asked.

"Like you're plotting your counter attack."

Since that was exactly what he was doing, he made no reply.

"I am not your enemy, Bear," she informed him.

"Then what are you? Because I can't seem to figure it out," he replied.

"Maybe I'm your next objective," she said, tossing another piece of fruit into her mouth. Did she do that on purpose to draw his attention to her lips? If so, she was a tactical genius because it was working beautifully. If he kissed her now, she would taste like mango.

"No." Not brilliant, but it was all that came to is mind while it was filled with thoughts of mango-lush lips.

She gave a little shrug, thrilled she was so obviously getting to him. He sighed.

She laughed.

He smiled, and the tension dispelled completely as she leaned forward to feed him a piece of mango, the last.

"I love the taste of mango," she said, now staring at his lips.

"Yep," he agreed, darting to his feet. "Ready? We'll arrive at the base today, if all goes well."

She squinted up at him. He scowled down at her. "No sabotage," he warned.

"It's uncanny how well you know me," she said. "Fine." She stood, tossed the mango pit into the trees, and dusted her hands. John rolled the hammock and packed his bag. From waking to walking, they were ready in three minutes.

"You amaze me, Juni. You look like the kind of woman who would be fussy and high maintenance, but here you are three days without a bath, hardly any food, traipsing through the jungle, and not a word of complaint." He shook his head in wonder.

"Some might say I'm the ideal woman for a rugged soldier such as yourself," she said.

"Who exactly might say that?" he asked.

"It might interest you to know people back home said it all the time. Hardly a day went by that someone didn't say, 'Boy, when that John Caruthers comes home from the army, he's going to have himself mighty fine girl in you, Juniper Dunbar.'"

John knew the town too well to doubt it was true. "And how long did it take them to stop saying that?"

"They said it until…" She gazed into the distance and gave a little shudder she tried to pass off as a shrug. "Until everyone realized you weren't coming home, I suppose. Took a long time. For all of us."

They walked in silence a few minutes.

"Bear." She reached out and clasped his hand, holding it in a companionable gesture similar to when they were kids. Juniper used to love to let their arms swing between them, the higher the better. "Didn't you think about us at all these many years? Didn't you think about *me*?"

"I know you want the answer to be yes, Juni. I know you want me to say I thought about you Dunbars all the time and stayed away for some odd reason you couldn't understand. But the truth is that I didn't. Not once, not at all."

"Oh." A few seconds later she withdrew her hand. He stopped short and turned her to face him, resting his hands on her shoulders.

"Not because I didn't care. More because I did. I had to cut things and people out of my life or else I wouldn't have survived the separation. Do you understand?"

She reached out and began to toy with a button on his chest, staring at it. "Did you think about anyone? Did anyone make the cut? Was anyone allowed to stay in your life, in your heart?"

"Ben and I still keep in touch, but it's sporadic. He's a soldier, too. He understands how it is. We see each other when we see each other and talk when we can talk. Otherwise no. I'm all alone in the world, and that's how I like it. I don't have anyone to miss and no one will miss me when I'm gone."

Her eyes flew to his and she pressed her palms on his chest. "Maybe that's still true for your part, John, but not for mine. I would miss you. If you died, a part of me would die with you."

"Don't say that, Juniper. I don't like it."

"Not liking it doesn't make it not true. You are a part of me, indelibly and forever. The connections you make when you're a child are the ones that last. Maybe that's not true for you, but it's true for me."

"You have so much better in your life than me. Why would you want to hang on to a battle-scarred soldier like me?" he asked. He honestly couldn't fathom the draw on her part. Surrounded by her loving, affectionate, boisterous family, why would she glom onto him, of all people? It was irrational, almost bizarre.

"I know exactly who and what you are, John Caruthers. And that's exactly why I'll never let go. Not ever. Not in a million years. There's nothing you can do to shake me, to push me away, to snuff out my affection."

He scowled at her, almost panicked by her words. If he could, he would run away, he who never ran away from anything. He had spent his entire career running toward gunfire, toward bombs, toward enemy combatants and almost certain death. What was it about this wisp of a girl with curly blond hair, a too-deep dimple, and intelligent hazel eyes who made him want to dodge into the jungle and take cover?

"And what about this boy you're set to marry? How does he figure into the equation?"

"Regardless of what you believe, I'm a realist. I understand the chances here aren't great. I want to be a wife and mother. Gabe is the best I've found, present company excluded. He's a good man, honest and upright. If I marry him, you'll move to that part of my heart reserved for family. Because you're also that. You're my past and…and I want you to be my future. But if you won't give me that, you still won't go away. I'll still hound you, still send you Christmas cards, still try to be with you on holidays. The point I'm trying to make is that I'm never going away, Bear. Never, ever. It's up to you in what capacity we co-exist from this point forward."

He cupped her face in his hands. "You talk like a scientist."

"That's because I am," she said, tipping forward on her toes to lean into his touch.

"No. You're far too adorable to be anything but Juniper Dunbar. You have been and will always be that little girl with the wild curls, holding on to my shirttail, urging me to pick her up, to go faster, to climb higher, to swim deeper."

Instead of heartening her, his words seemed to wound. He saw it reflected in eyes that rounded with pain. "Is that what this is about? You really still see me as a girl? You can't see me as a woman?"

"If you could see yourself through my eyes, you would understand once and forever the problem does not lie with you." He kissed her forehead.

"You vex me."

"Welcome to the club." He reached for his shirt and began to take it off. She stuttered and stared.

"Uh, what club exactly?"

"The jungle is thinning, meaning visibility is better, meaning I'm an easier target. Time to change out of my fatigues so it appears we're a honeymoon couple or some such."

"My lands," she said as he peeled off his shirt and reached into his bag for another.

"You quit thinking what you're thinking," he said. He wasn't modest. Living among so many men for the past decade had erased any chance of that. Group latrines and showers were a foregone conclusion in most cases. But no one had ever looked at him the way Juniper was now looking at him. It was enough to make him blush.

"How do you know what I'm thinking?" she asked, eyes riveted on his rippled abs.

"I can't say for sure, but I know it's enough to have your brain washed out with soap," he said.

"Don't be ridiculous. I'm a proper lady." He tugged the shirt down and she gave him a round of applause. "Encore."

"You quit that," he said, tossing his dirty shirt at her. She caught it and brought it to her nose, inhaling deeply.

"What on earth has got into you? There can't be anything pleasant about that stinky, sweaty shirt."

"That's a matter of opinion," she said. "But this," she waved toward his body, "is fact. You look like you've been chiseled from granite, Bear. What on earth do they do to you to make you look like that?"

"My lands, woman. Get yourself together." He heard the overt accent in his voice and couldn't seem to care. With Juniper, he didn't have to hide his past, his upbringing, his shameful history. There was more freedom in that than he realized there would be. "Let's head out."

They stepped into the clearing and stopped short again, unable to believe the sight that greeted them.

CHAPTER 19

"Look at that," Juniper breathed. They stood at the edge of a massive field of poppies, thousands upon thousands of them. "Poppies." She tugged John's shirt.

"I see," he said. His eyes squinted over the poppies to the trees beyond, scanning for people or danger.

"Aren't they beautiful?" Juniper said.

"Opium," Bear said, finally turning his eyes to the flowers. "They're grown for opium."

"Poppies are used for opium?" She faked a gasp. "I had no idea."

"Oh, that's right. You're a botanist," he said, booping her on the nose.

"I know they're used for ill purposes, but look at them and tell me they're beautiful," she demanded, hands on hips.

He shrugged.

She put her arm around his waist and turned him to face the field of flowers. "Clear your mind of crime and danger, of drugs and drug lords. Look at these flowers and see the beauty, the majesty, the amazing miracle of nature."

He studied the field, squinting intently, then picked her up and set her in front of him, in his line of vision. "Now I'm starting to see it."

"Oh, my lands." She pressed her hands to her cheeks. "What else are you hiding beneath that no-nonsense exterior, Mr. Romance?"

"Come here and find out," he said. Reaching for her hand, he pulled her close and led her in a dance. As with everything physical, he was a perfect lead, turning her and pulling her close again while she watched in wide-eyed amazement.

After he showed off his skills for a bit with the foxtrot, he pulled her close and slipped both arms around her, swaying gently.

"We're trampling thousands of dollars worth of opium here," he said.

"Totally worth it. And guess what?"

"What?" he asked, preemptively smiling at whatever she was about to say.

"Poppies are my new favorite flower."

"Quite a distinction, coming from a botanist."

"I'll say," she agreed.

"Guess what?" he said.

"What?" she asked, and now she was the one who smiled in anticipation of what he was about to say.

"Poppies are my new favorite flower, too."

"Quite a distinction, coming from a major."

"I'll say."

They swayed in comfortable silence a while longer, saying things with their eyes they dared not say with their lips. "Where and when did you learn to dance like that? Don't tell me the army taught you."

"In a manner of speaking. For anyone on the kind of career track I'm on, dance lessons are highly recommended. Never know when you might get called up to a political or diplomatic to-do."

"You are ever full of surprises, John Caruthers," she said.

"No, I am forever the same and unchanging," he said.

"That's what gets me. You are consistent, and yet unexpected. Tough, yet tender. Hard, yet soft. Strong, yet gentle."

"I don't think many people would agree with you on those second points, Juni," he said.

"They don't know the things I know, haven't been privy to the things I've seen and observed. I remember...I remember when you told me about your dog."

He felt like he swallowed a handful of toothpicks, all of a sudden. "You were so little. You can't possibly remember." She was only four when he blurted the story of his dog. It was his mother's birthday and he felt unusually sentimental. As ever, Juniper was his constant companion. He had grown so comfortable with her that he sometimes had the habit of talking out loud, as if to himself, forgetting her little listening ears. He told her about his dog. He shouldn't have. It wasn't a story for children; it wasn't a story for anyone. But talking to Juniper had become its own sort of therapy and it came spilling out of him that day.

"But I do remember. I remember every word. His name was Pal. He was a shepherd mix mutt your dad brought home from the road one day."

He shook his head, not wanting her to continue, but she pressed on, either oblivious or stubborn.

"He was your constant companion, your best friend. He slept on your floor each night, guarding you, comforting you when your parents fought. And then...and then your dad, well... Pal died."

John clutched the shirt at her waist, trying not to remember. Of all the horrible things that happened in his childhood, he had no idea why it was the worst memory. His mother had often been at his father's mercy, had been beaten and bruised. Why a dog's torturous death should rank higher than that didn't make sense. But perhaps it was because his mother had a choice in the matter and the dog hadn't. To this day, the sight of a dog made him sick and he had to look away.

"I remember your face the day you told me. It was the only day in our entire history together that I saw you so sad, so...vulnerable and human. I so badly wanted to help you, to fix you."

John remembered how she'd climbed in his lap, little arms hugging his neck tightly. That day for the first time, maybe for the only time, he hugged her back, pressing his face hard into her neck and squeezing in return. He'd forgotten, until now. Another memory blocked because he didn't want to believe it, didn't want to remember that he had once gotten something from his time with the Dunbars. It was easier for him to believe he'd been an unwilling participant in their family dynamic than to believe he'd walked away from an actual family who'd loved him, who he had loved in return.

"I'm quite a mess, Juniper," he declared.

"We're all a mess in our own way, Bear," she returned.

"You are not a mess. Look at you, so lovely and put together. A botanist, working on your own in your chosen field."

"I'm certain no one looking at you would guess what you've been through, either," she reminded him. "People only see what we want them to see. They only see the masks we put up." They were silent a while. Somewhere in there they'd stopped swaying. Instead they clung, hugging tightly, her ear on his heart, his head on hers. "You should get a dog."

"Can't," he said.

"Because you're gone too much or because it hurts too much?"

"Both," he reluctantly admitted. There was no sense in trying to tiptoe around the truth when she already knew it. Strangely, he didn't mind so much to have her peer into the painful parts of him, the parts he tried to keep hidden.

"This is where a wife would come in handy. She could keep the dog while you're away. Coincidentally, I love dogs."

He laughed and gave her a squeeze. "You're relentless."

"You already knew that about me."

"Yes, but I'd forgotten. I forgot a lot of things I shouldn't have, Juniper. I'm sorry about that. Sorry I hurt you, sorry I hurt your folks."

She eased back so she could see his face. "You were an eighteen-year-old kid, dealing with a lot of painful emotional scars."

"You're being awfully generous and forgiving," he noted.

"I wasn't finished. You were an eighteen-year-old hurting kid then, but you're a thirty-two-year old man now. What are you gonna do about it? Because it seems to me you have some lost years to make up for, to me especially. Starting now."

"You don't give up."

"Not ever," she said. "I happen to know a good thing when I see it and you, Major Caruthers, are the best thing I've ever found. Now, I want you to do something for me."

"What's that?" he asked. If she asked him to kiss her right now, he wasn't certain he had the strength to resist, nor that he wanted to.

"I want you to try and beat me to the other side." With a little smack to his bicep, she turned and took off.

John's competitive instinct roared to life. He set off, overtook her in three steps, then made the mistake of turning to look at her—hair streaming, face beaming. He stopped short and stood still while she sprinted past him, arms out, poppies all around her. He hadn't spent a lot of his time pondering artwork or photographs, but he wished then he had the talent and ability to capture the moment, not that he'd ever be able to forget.

Juniper stopped at the other side of the field, bent over and trying to catch her breath. John caught up with her slowly. When he reached her side, she straightened and tossed him a saucy smile.

"Does this confirm the fact that you're too old to win?" she asked.

"Maybe. Or maybe it confirms that I've finally found something I like better than winning," he said.

"And what might that be?" she asked.

"Juniper Dunbar, enjoying life."

"If I didn't know you better, I might think that was a line."

"Then knowing me as you do, you realize it's not. You are full in on life, Juni. Brimming with passion and joy. It's a sight to behold." He reached up and touched one of her curls. Her hair was tousled, as usual. And as usual she seemed not to notice. But he liked that about her. Juniper was more concerned with the actuality of living than the appearance of it. He picked up her hand and inspected her nails, confirming what he'd guessed. They were broken and jagged, stained from so many hours in the dirt and touching tree bark and sap.

"You're staring at my fingers a disconcerting amount. You can't keep them, you know. I need them."

"I would, if I could," he said, bringing her hand to his cheek. He pressed it to his face. "I would keep every part of you tucked in my pocket and bring it out when I need a smile. Because you make me smile, Juniper, even when I don't want to. You make me remember there are good people in the world. You make me believe."

Far from being pleased by his words, she looked sad. "Just not enough."

They regarded each other in somber silence a moment, her unable to let go of the hope that he might unbend and let her in, him unable to convey how much he already had. Did she have no idea the changes she had already wrought in him? But he couldn't give her more. They had reached the end of the line.

He turned his back to her. "Hop on, I'll carry you the rest of the way."

"How far is it?" she asked. She hopped on his back and nestled her nose against his cheek, inhaling his scent while unconsciously bestowing her own.

"Not far enough," he said and, with an affectionate little pat to her arm, set off once again.

They strolled onto the Honduran army base at sunset. Or rather plodded. Neither was anxious nor happy to arrive, despite the fact that they were hungry and exhausted. True to his word, John had carried her the remaining way. Juniper could easily have walked on her own, but neither had wanted that. They wanted to cling together. Carrying her on his back gave them an excuse to do so. Now, at first sight of the base, she slid off and walked beside him in heavy silence.

They had only taken a few steps when they were greeted by soldiers with machine guns. Juniper tensed. John reached for her hand and gave it a squeeze. He opened his mouth to offer greeting, but the soldiers recognized him first, their attitudes changing so fast from machismo to fear that one of them literally dropped his gun and reached for it with shaking hands.

"Sir," they said, saluting.

"As you were, gentlemen."

"Your base radioed you'd be here yesterday, sir," the other said, a question in his tone. His brows rose as his gaze shifted to John's hand, still joined to Juniper's. He was never going to live this down. Somehow it was hard to care.

"And so we should have been, but we ran into some rebels and slowed our pace. We'll need a clean up crew," John replied. "Also Miss Dunbar will need a shower, some clothes, a room for the night, and some food."

"Sir?" the second man replied. The first still stared at him, trembling.

"I'm not certain which part of that was hard to understand, soldier," John said, and now the first one started to tremble as his gaze darted to Juniper and away.

"It's just that I was under the impression the young lady needed a transport, sir. One is leaving in ten minutes. But if you'd rather she not go…" his words trailed off and he paled, uncertain if he'd said too much.

Juniper tensed, and now so did John. "Of course I want her on that transport," he said. Juniper tried to withdraw her hand, but he wouldn't allow it. "If you could give us a few minutes."

"Yes, sir," the braver man said, then both men darted away.

"They're most certainly going to change their underpants. Honestly, John, the effect you have on people."

"Too much?" he asked, now facing her.

"I think it's magnificent," she said in a hushed whisper, as if it were a shameful confession. "I love that you're terrifying to everyone but me."

He did too, if he were being honest.

She clutched the hem of her shirt, twisting her fingers nervously in the material smile fading. "Bear."

"Juniper."

"Don't make me beg."

"The Juniper Dunbar I know wouldn't begin to know how," he replied.

"I didn't used to think so, but…" She took a breath. "Pl…"

He pressed his thumb to her lips and shook his head. "Let me tell you something, Juni. You know I would kill for you, I've already done it. I would also die for you, in a heartbeat, no hesitation. But I have no idea how to live for you, none whatsoever. I'm not a husband or father."

"You could be," Juniper said. "I can see it, Bear. I can see it so clearly. You would be amazing at it."

"I would be a giant question mark, always with the potential to be a disaster. I can't do that to you, not when a more certain life awaits you."

Her eyes filled with tears and it was like a knife through his heart. "Will you at least kiss me goodbye?"

"No. I can't."

"Why? So I won't have to tell my fiancé I cheated?"

"What you tell that boy is up to you. I can't kiss you for a selfish reason—because I can't risk knowing what I can't have. I'm an all-or-nothing person, either all in or all out. I can't straddle the middle, and especially not with you."

"So I'm nothing, is that what you're telling me?" The tears spilled over and eased down her face.

"You are everything," he said, picking her up and holding her impossibly close. He buried his face in her hair while she pressed her face to his neck.

"Bear, I love you so."

He wouldn't, couldn't say anything in return. The lack irritated her. She eased away and scowled into his face.

"You have ruined me, do you know that? You have ruined me for anyone else."

He blinked down at her, shocked. "I haven't touched you."

She barked a harsh laugh. "Is that what you think? You have left your mark on me, indelibly and forever and I just…wanted and expected so much more from you." She wriggled and he set her down. She took a step back and they regarded each other. He had the sense she was giving him one final chance. He wouldn't, couldn't open his mouth, mostly because he didn't trust what might come out.

"Sir? Pardon the interruption, but the transport is ready. If the young lady is ready?"

John forced himself to take a step back. He thought it would probably be the hardest step he would ever have to take. Juniper's face didn't crumple, but she did cry harder, tears that had once been a slow drizzle now a tsunami that covered her entire face. The soldier fished in his pocket and handed her a tissue.

"Thank you," she murmured, summoning a smile that, even in his misery, sent a dagger of jealousy shuddering through John. The only way he could survive, could resist reaching for her, was to stand at ease, to remind himself he was a soldier and duty came first, even when he didn't want it to.

She turned and walked away without a word, shoulders back and proud. Only someone who really knew her, as he admitted he did, could tell how wounded she was and how hard she was trying to keep it together. She would likely cry all the way back to the states. John envied her that. For the first time since he was a child, he wished he hadn't lost the ability to cry. It would feel wonderfully freeing to rid himself of the weight of everything now pressing on his chest.

Of course part of that weight wasn't due to sadness or longing. He stumbled, bumping the soldier who remained with him. The man regarded him curiously. It was the terrified man from before, who finally found his words.

"Sir? Are you all right?"

"In a moment, Private," John said. He remained facing Juniper until she was long out of sight. Though he couldn't see it, he knew she'd boarded the plane by now. He could hear the engine and waited until it took off, until it was gone from view, and then he spoke.

"Private."

"Yes, sir."

"Radio the on-base medic and tell him I have need of his services."

"Sir? Are you ill?"

"No, I'm shot." He stumbled again and the man grabbed onto him, tentatively at first, then taking more of his weight when John sagged into him.

The next few minutes were a bit of a blur as a medic was called, along with a Jeep for transport. The next time John was fully awake, he was in the sick bay, the medic staring worriedly down at him.

"Sir," the medic said. "When did this happen?" He motioned to the tidy hole in John's chest.

"A couple of days ago." The first Sandinista, Juniper's captor with the gun, might have died happy if he'd realized one of his wayward shots had found its target. It wasn't the first time John had been shot, though he'd never been shot in the chest before. He at first thought it was a good thing the wound didn't bleed, had barely made a hole. He'd been able to convince himself that maybe he hadn't been shot; maybe one of the bullets splintered or it was an errant piece of shrapnel from one of the surrounding trees, maybe the world's largest splinter. It was so tiny Juniper hadn't even noticed it when she watched him change. In any case he'd had other things to do and focus on, no time for an injury. But as time waned, the feeling in his chest became heavier, each breath harder to achieve. When the little hole became angry, red, and hot, he knew he was headed for trouble. Bacteria loved the warm, moist air of the jungle. He had been mostly certain he would make it to base, and he was more than glad he'd hadn't had to tell Juniper, to add his injury to everything else they'd had to deal with.

"You're going to need surgery, sir. We're sending you stateside," the medic said.

John sighed, frustrated. "Is that absolutely necessary, Lieutenant? Can't you stitch me up here and send me back?"

The man blinked at him. "Sir, there's significant damage. I have no idea how you're still standing, let alone how you walked here under your own steam. I'm sorry, sir, but I can't handle this. I...I'm not even certain you'll make the flight, if I'm being honest. This is beyond me. This is astonishingly serious."

"Fine." The man faded from view. John squinted, trying to keep him in focus before he lost consciousness again. "No general anesthetic."

"Sir..."

John snapped at him, a literal snap of fingers because words were becoming too precious. "Not my rule, son. I know too much. No general..." Oh, no, did he slur? How embarrassing.

"Yes, sir," the medic said, sounding longsuffering. Or maybe worried.

"No opioids," John added. "Poppies…" he murmured. His head tipped to the right and it was the last vision he had before everything went black again, Juniper, standing in a field of poppies, her arms held out beseechingly toward him.

CHAPTER 21

In a surprise to absolutely no one, The Major was a terrible patient. After they stabilized him at the base in Honduras, they flew him—unconscious—to Bethesda, Maryland where he had surgery. Though he was given only local anesthetic, he was still unconscious for the procedure, a fact he did not mind at all. When he came to, there was a tube down his throat he quickly yanked out. That got him a verbal tongue lashing from one of the nurses. The worst part of that was that his throat hurt too much to reply.

For two days he lay in silent misery. The pain annoyed him, but it was manageable. He hadn't gotten where he was in life by allowing pain to slow him. Inactivity and helplessness, though. Those were the silent killers. He did not want to be in a hospital, least of all in a bed. And then there were the nurses.

They scurried around him looking petrified. He had no idea why, unless word had spread about him. So far he had refrained from yelling at any of them, realizing they were simply doing their jobs. Maybe he glared a bit, but if they knew how much restraint he showed by not lashing out, they would be warmer and friendlier, not dash by his doorway like he was the boogeyman and any sighting might turn them to stone.

Juniper wouldn't be afraid.

And then there were those unwanted thoughts, provided by his traitorous brain. Apparently it hadn't gotten the memo that they were letting go of Juniper because it kept providing thoughts and memories about her every few seconds. It had made a new game of comparing every other woman he encountered to her. Unsurprisingly, every other woman came up short. But it was true: Juniper would not be afraid of him, would not speak in hushed whispers or spill the water because her hands were shaking from being in the same room with him. She would tell him exactly like it was, and then she would take care of him, far better than these mousy women ever could. Perhaps she would crawl into bed beside him and...

He forced his brain to cut off that line of thought, as he had been doing every time it began. His entire miserable existence now revolved around lying in bed, ignoring the pain in his chest, ignoring the thoughts in his head, ignoring the pangs in his heart.

On the third day he stood, yanked all attachments from his body, got dressed, and walked out of the hospital.

"You can't go," one of the bolder nurses yelled at him, trotting to keep up in her squishy nurse shoes.

"Watch me," he growled.

"You'll be AMA. You'll get court martialed," she threatened, at which point he stopped short and whirled to face her.

She stopped short, too, nearly toppling over in her haste to avoid a collision. "What did you say, Lieutenant?"

A shudder ran through her, and she seemed to rethink her hasty threat. "With all due respect, sir. You haven't been released."

"I'm releasing myself," he said.

"That's not how it works," she said, stamping her squishy foot on the concrete. "Major, please come back inside before you catch cold."

He looked around, realizing for the first time it was winter in the states, and cold. A southern boy, he'd never acclimated to cold weather. Still, he didn't care. He was done with the hospital, hopefully forever. Next time he set foot in one, he'd better be dead. "Lieutenant, no."

"But…" she began, annoyed in the extreme with his disobedience. "You're not done yet."

"I'm done. I am so done. Don't worry, I'll clear it with my superior officer."

"Who is your superior officer?" she demanded.

He waved her away and turned his back on her. He was at that stage where he didn't have many, which was both a comfort and a concern. The buck crept closer and closer to stopping with him. "As you were, Lieutenant."

"Major. *Major*," she screeched. "I know what you're wearing. *You don't even have underpants.*"

That shouldn't have made him laugh, but it did. And, again, it reminded him of Juniper. She would find it hilarious, would dimple and giggle and probably fall over from laughing, as she did whenever she laughed too hard. *I'll have to tell her next time I see her,* he thought, and scowled. He wouldn't see her. Once again he'd have to purge himself of Alabama and home and people. He'd done it once before. Why did the prospect of doing it now hurt so badly?

I need closure. It was one of those newfangled words the army psychologists were always trying to foist on him. *The men need closure, closure from their injuries, their assignments, their families.* John thought it was all ridiculous nonsense. What the men needed was to grow up and be men, to stop coddling their blasted feelings all the livelong day and embrace their assignments. And he was no different. He did not need *closure.* He needed to repay a debt, to settle an old score. He owed the Dunbars, both an explanation and his gratitude. He was overdue on both. And if he happened to catch word about Juniper's whereabouts while he was there, so be it. It wasn't like he was looking for her, not specifically. He was merely making good on his word.

With that decided, he caught a taxi and went straight to the airport, not bothering to stop and grab clean underpants. *What they don't know won't hurt them.* And absolutely no one would know the state of his undergarments, or lack thereof. Life was easier when he traveled lightly, both with clothes and people. He'd see the Dunbars, cross that from his list, and then he could get back to doing what he did best—being alone.

ohn had no idea what to expect when he reached his former hometown. He didn't know if it would look the same, smell the same, *feel* the same. He hadn't hated the town. He'd hated who he was when he was there, hated the weight of shame and pity that followed him everywhere he went. But the people had always been kind. No one said anything in his presence. Perhaps they didn't say anything behind his back, but he doubted it. Knowing how small towns worked, he thought he was the object of speculation wherever he went.

He could never tell if being with the Dunbars had elevated his status or made him more of a spectacle. To be sure, being the lone orphaned survivor of a scandalous murder-suicide was bad. But had it been better to be the ward of those loony Dunbars? Though they had been liked and respected, they hadn't fit in, not by far. Dustin Dunbar was the only PhD for miles, had more education than most of the town put together. He hadn't put on airs or held himself above anyone. On the contrary, he'd been warm and friendly, overtly outgoing. But he'd been different, nonetheless. He was the quintessential absent minded professor, always wearing a sport coat and carrying a book, usually with a child or three in tow whenever he ran errands in town. And the children hadn't fit, either. Most of the locals were farmers, meaning their children were farm children—hale, hardy, and hard-working. All of the Dunbars had a dreamy quality about them. You could tell whenever you met them that their heads were in the clouds. They talked about things no one else could understand—high literature and philosophy, routinely weaving those topics into everyday conversation so the neighboring farm children stared at them like they were from another planet. John used to, too, before he lived with them. He used to pile on with the other children, rolling his eyes at *Those Dunbars.*

And then he became one, and it was no longer weird to discuss Plato at lunch and Dante at supper. The more enmeshed he became with the Dunbars, the more people in town started to look at him differently. From pity and suspicion to awe and respect. *He's one of them now, educated and high-minded.*

The Dunbars had to know they didn't fit, but they never let on. It would have been easy for them to keep themselves apart from everyone, to not rub shoulders with the uneducated rabble in the town. But they hadn't. They had immersed themselves in every aspect of town life, from church to funerals to everything in between. Juniper's mother, Jane Dunbar, was an excellent cook and baker. For her, that was enough of an entrée to be accepted. She provided cookies and pies and cakes for every major event. Dustin was so outgoing and affable, people ended up loving him, even if they couldn't understand most of what he said. His mind was on another plane, but his heart was big and pure and people responded to it.

They were really quite a wonder, John realized as he drove through town and saw how much everything looked the same. That they had chosen this place and made a home for themselves among humble farm people was a testament to their character. Dustin could have gone somewhere like Oxford or Cambridge. He had that kind of mind, a brilliant one. But he hadn't wanted that kind of life, for him or his children. He'd had the wisdom to understand he wanted to be surrounded by real people who did real living, salt of the earth people. People like John and his family.

I had the best of both worlds, he thought. He'd been raised by blue collar parents, bestowing values like hard work and a stoic, uncomplaining nature. And then he'd been given a glimpse into the other world, the thinking man's world. And he'd absorbed Dustin's ability to see the world as a whole, to make all the parts come together. Dustin had loved the symmetry of everything, had routinely pointed out to his brood the mathematics of everyday life. Literally he saw the Fibonacci sequence in everything. For him music wasn't merely music —it was the ultimate combination of mathematics and poetry. He had taught his children to see the world that way, with all the parts tangled up together, John included.

He intended to go straight to the Dunbars', certain their house would also be exactly as it was. But the cemetery caught his interest instead. He parked and walked the familiar path to his parents' gravestone, pausing to regard it. He stooped and cleared a few weeds from the edges of his mother's side and then lingered in a crouch, staring at the date. It was and would always be the worst day of his life, but it hadn't been an ending. It had been a new beginning, at least for him. Living with the Dunbars had started him on a new trajectory, his current path. Without that awful event, he wouldn't be where he now was. And he liked where he was, who he was. Reconnecting with Juniper had shown him a lot of things, namely that he wasn't as broken as he'd always believed. He was a soldier, yes, and sometimes he had to do things because of that. But he wasn't half a man as he'd always thought. He hadn't died that day with his parents, hadn't lost the ability to love or be loved in return. He'd merely chosen to put it away for the sake of his career.

Is that still what you choose?

It was a terrifying question, and the first time he'd ever asked it of himself. What if...

But no. He had already chosen. No need to revisit that choice. He was a soldier for life, for however long he had left. Let Juniper have her life with her family and her scientist. She would no doubt be happier that way, living with people who could love her and be loved in return, with people who could be *there*. Even if John miraculously healed the mangled parts of him, he would still spend most of his life away. That was no way for her to live, on her own, always waiting and wondering if he'd come back again.

He blinked, seeing his parents' tombstone again. If the Dunbars were there, they would encourage him to say something to them, but he couldn't. It wasn't within him to speak to the dead. But he had come, had showed up and paid his respects. That was something, he supposed. And he had put to rest some old ghosts. Juniper helped him see things anew, to give his mother the respect she was due. For so long John had blamed her for being weak, for remaining with his father. But what choice did she have? She with an eighth grade education and no skills, save homemaking. Where would they have gone? How would she have supported him? And then there was her last act of bravery and courage. Of *love.* She had done the best for him she could, with what she had to work with. He could now forgive her the weakness and admire the bravery, could appreciate all the love, affection, and protection she gave him. He gave the cold stone a gentle pat and stood, turning and walking away. It was likely he would never come back, and that was okay. He had put old ghosts to rest. He had found *closure.*

He grimaced, shaking off the thought. Surely there had to be a better word, one that did not put him on level ground with the mealy mouthed little psychologist they were always foisting on him. *Dustin will know the exact word,* he thought and felt a sudden urgency to see the surrogate father he hadn't seen in fourteen years. Picking up the pace, he practically trotted to his car, heading toward the Dunbars. Heading toward *home.*

CHAPTER 22

He drove up the long lane to their house, heart thrumming. They lived on a little farm. Not that they ever grew anything, minus the herbs Jane grew for cooking. But the land and barn had given them space to raise all the animals they rescued—goats, dogs, children. Over the years they had fostered other kids. John was the only one who stuck.

Though not fancy, it was a vast improvement over the rundown little house of his first twelve years. They'd had acres of land, with woods and a stream. There had always been a fresh kitten, lamb, goat kid, or baby llama to play with and enjoy. There were also dogs, but John had avoided those, the memory of his own lost dog too fresh and painful. *I think I'm ready for another dog,* he thought, the unexpected thought jolting him with surprise. He had told himself he would never have another dog, and here he was, thinking about one again. Amazing how he had spent six years with the Dunbars and hadn't unfrozen at all, and then spent a few days with Juniper and unbent completely. What made the difference?

He was so immersed in his thoughts it took him a minute to realize the farmhouse was dark and still, two things that never happened in relation to the Dunbars. Even when they were away the lights were on. He could blame it on an errant child, but Dustin had been the worst offender. Somehow it had fallen to John to be the last one out because he was the one most prone to turning everything off.

More than the darkness and silence, the house had an overgrown, unlived in feel to it. In fact the grass was knee high, weeds creeping around the foundation. Jane Dunbar never would have allowed that. Though he knew it was fruitless, John parked the car, got out, and peeked in the windows of the house.

Empty, barren, and had been for some time.

He stood on the porch, overlooking the vast yard, as wave upon wave of memory rushed to greet him. The house had been pure chaos, had felt like too much to a traumatized, closed off kid. But now, in retrospect, the memories were sweet, as were the feelings they evoked. He could almost hear the noise of children laughing, running, yelling, singing. Could almost smell the culinary delights emerging from Jane's kitchen. Could practically see Juniper toddling up to him, arms aloft to be picked up. Why had he fought so hard against all of it when, at this moment, he would give anything for even a taste of it?

He sank to the front porch step and had a visceral, eerily real vision of Juniper approaching, dead frog clutched to her chest. *Fix it, Bear.* The frog had been so far gone it was practically mummified, squished and desiccated. But her face had been so earnest, so sad that he'd wished for some sort of wizardry to make the frog whole again, if only to make her smile. *I can't, Juni. It's gone.*

Gone? What do you mean gone? It's right there.

It died.

What is 'died'?

It went away forever; it won't come back.

Like your Mama and Daddy?

Yes, like that, he'd replied, tone solemn and somber.

Juniper had studied him a few beats, then taken the frog out of his grasp and replaced it with herself, snuggling close, wrapping her little arms around his neck. She hadn't been able to stand it when he was sad, had done everything in her power to try and fix him.

Some things never change, he thought, picking up a rock and tossing it absently. His glance slid to his rental car, the desire to pick up the adult version of Juniper and hold her close almost overpowering him. Had coming here been a mistake? He wasn't sure what to do next. The feeling of uncertainty unnerved him, but it was more than that. Why hadn't Juniper mentioned that the family had moved? And how was it possible they had? He had pictured them in this same house, carrying on as ever, possibly into eternity.

A bit of rational thought returned and he berated himself. *Did you really think you would change and they wouldn't?* It had been fourteen years and all their children left home. Perhaps they moved into town, where there was less yard work. Maybe they moved somewhere else to be with one of their kids. Knowing them, they would be far flung, possibly even in other countries, if Juniper was any indication. They weren't the sort of people who grew up and settled in their hometown; they were the sort who were launched into some interesting and creative new life.

One thing was certain: the people in town would know where they went. It wasn't the nature of town to keep things private. Everything was everyone's business. Strangely, John had never minded that. It seemed like the kind of thing he would, private as he was. Somehow he had accepted it as an intrinsic part of small town living, perhaps because it had always worked to his benefit. People had always been kind to him, extra kind, he thought. First because they knew what was going on in his home, and then because they knew how it ended up.

Unlike the Dunbars' closed up homestead, the town looked exactly the same. There was even still a General Store on Main Street, the last of a dying breed. John parked and entered the store, steeling himself for glances, stares, and whispers.

Only one person was in the store, and he let out his breath. "John Caruthers, as I live and breathe." The store's owner, Mr. Elswick, spoke from his ubiquitous spot behind the counter.

"Sir," John said, tipping his head in a respectful little nod.

"Look at you, all growed up and some kind of soldier. A major, last we heard. Course we all knew you'd turn out good."

"Then you had better knowledge than I did, sir," John replied.

Mr. Elswick chuckled. "It couldn't have gone any other way, what with how Dustin Dunbar used to brag on you."

"Sir?"

"There was hardly a time he came in my store that he didn't talk about you. 'That John Caruthers has a fine mind. You keep an eye on him, he's going to go somewhere and do something great.' You'da thought you were his natural born son, so proud was he of you."

John's throat felt uncomfortably tight and he cleared it. "Thank you, sir. That's actually why I'm here. I went to the Dunbars' homestead and found it empty. I wonder if you might know where they've gone."

Mr. Elswick blinked at him, a deer in headlights expression. "Why, haven't you heard?"

"No, sir," John prompted, chest kicking with sudden anxiety. Maybe they'd gone to New York. That would certainly make a local look as panicked and heartsick as Mr. Elswick now looked. He scratched his temple and took a deep breath, letting it out in a heavy huff.

"I thought for sure somebody would have tracked you down. Juniper tried, God love her. When she disappeared, too, we assumed…" He motioned helplessly to John who took a step forward and gripped the counter between them.

"Mr. Elswick, what happened to the Dunbars?"

Mr. Elswick took another breath. When he let it out this time it sounded wet and rheumy, filled with sickness or sadness. Maybe both. "They died, John."

John blinked at him, disbelieving. "Dustin and Jane died?"

Mr. Elswick shook his head. "All of them, every last one but Juniper. They were going to visit her in college for some award or something. In that big van of theirs, you know the one. A drunk driver crossed the median in the highway. Dustin lingered for a couple days, but then…" He paused and shook his head. "Poor little Juniper, the weight of all that, all those burials. We all helped how we could, mind, but she wasn't the same after that. She got it in her head to find you, went all the way to West Point. And that was the last we heard. I take it she never found you. That's a pity. Poor little thing. She was always so bright and cheerful. I hate to think what this has done to her." He shook his head and bowed it.

John remained staring at him in silence, fists clenched on the counter. His first reaction was rage, white hot rage. The Dunbars… gone. All of them. Killed by a drunk driver. He wanted to pound his fists into…something. Surely not the old man in front of him, nor his beloved store. But *something*. Something had to take the brunt of his anger.

"The man who killed them," John choked. Perhaps it wasn't too late to track him down and kill him.

"Died. His car went up in a fireball. Thankfully that didn't happen to the Dunbars, but… It was bad, son. It was bad." He shook his head again. Slowly, sadly. He must have noted John's stricken expression because his became stricken, too. He cleared his throat. "I'm awful sorry, son. Sorry to be the one to tell you, sorry it happened, sorry you lost them after losing your own folks. If only you could find Juniper, offer her some comfort. I'm sure she'd sore appreciate it, her all alone in the world now."

John swallowed down waves of rage and revulsion. He felt like everything he'd ever eaten was about to come back up, but he wouldn't let it. He sucked a deep breath and stuck out his hand for a shake. "I do appreciate you telling me, sir. Thank you for that, and for keeping an eye on me when I was young. One time you gave my mother an extra two cans of soup. I've never forgotten. I thank you for your kindness."

Mr. Elswick blinked at him, shocked and a bit overwhelmed and embarrassed. "Oh, well, it weren't nothing. Your mother was a fine lady and a good soul. You, too. You done this town proud, done your mother and the Dunbars proud, too. They never stopped loving you, used to talk kindly about you right up until the end. We all rather thought you and Juniper… That is to say… When she went searching for you… Well, it seemed like it would have been a good thing, you and her together. But last I heard she got herself engaged to some city slicker. I hope he's a good one. She deserves it."

"Yes, sir, she certainly does. Thank you, sir. You have a good day."

"You too, son. Take care."

John gave him a nod, walked out of the store, around the corner into the alley, bent over, and heaved until his stomach was empty, then heaved again for good measure. He rested his forehead against the brick, trying to breathe through the sudden heaviness in his chest. The Dunbars gone, all of them. Juniper all alone, and she hadn't said a word. Or had she? *I tried so hard to find you. I needed you. Can you just hold me? I'm so tired, John.* And his response to her pain had been to laugh at her, to condescend and tell her she was too young and sheltered to know anything about suffering. He'd sent her back into the world with the knowledge that she'd be safe in the shelter of her family. Instead he'd sent her back into the world alone, unprotected, *unloved.*

He straightened and blinked. *No. Absolutely no.* Juniper Dunbar alone and unloved was too ridiculous a prospect to even speculate. It would not, could not happen, not on his watch.

Seemingly John had been born in need of a mission. The army had given him many of those over the years, along with great purpose. But now he'd found his own objective. Nothing had ever been more important, more urgent, or more necessary than the one now running through his mind: *Find Juniper Dunbar.*

With no time to lose, he hopped in his car and drove away, leaving dust trails in his haste to get started.

Las Vegas. Knowing Juniper as he did, John should have guessed she would have some sort of knee-jerk reaction to his rejection. *I'll show him*, he could almost hear her thinking it as she returned from Honduras—humiliated and angry—and called up her erstwhile fiancé. *Lets' get married, the sooner the better. We'll elope. How's next weekend?* Now here he was, and the most he could say for the grimy, debauched place was that it was hot, unlike DC had been.

He stared through the peephole of the door. Not the most dignified entrance, but he needed to know something before he entered.

Juniper and the fiancé stood at the front of the room, a preacher between them. The man looked about like John imagined he would, like the sort of man who worked with his head instead of his hands for his living—well-dressed with wire-rimmed glasses. Juniper, on the other hand, was spectacle-free. John squinted, staring hard at her face. She glanced at her watch, then at the clock, and that was when he saw it, or rather the lack of it. Juniper's face, lacking her telltale dimple.

John wasn't one for dramatic entrances. But that missing dimple was his undoing. He kicked the door open, fighting a wince when it banged hard against the wall, echoing through the small room.

"I object," he called, loud enough for his voice to carry and reverberate.

"We haven't gotten to that part yet," the preacher said. "We just got started."

"Well, I still object," John said, walking forward. Now he stood before the duo and across from the preacher. "We can do this the easy way or the hard way."

"Easy way," the preacher said. His bored tone told everyone it probably wasn't the first time he'd had such an encounter.

"Hard way," Juniper said, hands on hips. Her dimple flashed, in annoyance, but the sight made John smile.

"I'll split the difference. Hard way for you, easy for them," he assured her. He faced the two men. "I'm sorry about this. Maybe someday we can sit down like gentlemen and discuss it." To the preacher he added. "Sorry to desecrate the holiness of this tacky chapel."

"Who is this guy?" the still unknown fiancé asked, tone full of sufficient outrage.

"Bear," Juniper said, outrage matching her fiancé's.

The man's eyes bugged. "That's Bear? You said he was old."

"He is," Juniper said, stamping her foot.

"Fine, just for that," John said and tossed her over his shoulder.

"Wait, what is going on?" the fiancé asked as John began carrying Juniper back down the aisle.

"None of your concern," John told him. "Mind your business."

"I'll call you," Juniper said.

"Oh, no, you won't," John contradicted, resisting the almost overpowering urge to smack her on the behind when it was so easily within his reach.

They reached the outside and he tucked her safely in his car. Juniper crossed her arms over her chest and regarded him in silence until he slid behind the wheel.

"Where are your glasses?" he demanded.

"Is that really the first thing you say to me after you force carry me out of my wedding?" she asked.

He quirked an eyebrow, waiting her out.

"I got contacts," she said, tossing her hands wide. "Bear..."

"Wait. If we talk here, we're going to broil. Plus there's the chance your boyfriend could come outside. I made it thus far without breaking his nose, I'd like to see it through."

She re-crossed her arms and glowered. John drove through the streets of Las Vegas, eventually parking in the shade of a tall building. It wasn't cool by any means, but it was better than being in direct sunlight. He left the car running for the air, put it in park, and faced her.

They squared off, waiting to see who would break first. Since he had, in fact, carried her out of her wedding, he figured he owed her one.

"I went home."

Her lashes fluttered furiously a few times. "Then I guess you know."

"I do. What I don't know is why you didn't tell me. How could you keep something like that from me, Juni?"

Her shoulders sagged. "I didn't want you to know."

"Why not?"

"Because I knew if you did, you'd do something like this. You'd come get me."

"I thought that was what you wanted," he said.

"Of course it was what I wanted. But not like this, not out of some sense of misplaced responsibility or, worse, pity."

"Huh," he said, studying her. The female mind was unfathomable to him, Juniper's especially. In Honduras she'd done nothing but tell him they should be together. And now here they were together and she said it wasn't right.

Her eyes filled with tears. She turned away to try and hide them, but too late. John took a shaky breath. The sight of those tears was worse than being shot. Slowly, tentatively, he reached across the console and stroked the soft curls at her temple, gently, *tenderly*. "How about if I came to get you because I don't want to go one more minute of my life without you?"

Her head swiveled in his direction, eyes luminous with unshed tears. She regarded him in wary silence, eyes skimming his face as if for clues. "I think I need a bit more explanation than that."

"Of course you do. I swear, Juniper, you find it physically impossible to let me take the easy way in life."

"You hate the easy way," she reminded him.

"I do, at that," he agreed happily. He took a breath. "I spent six years with your family, six years of daily hugs and I-love-yous and them trying their best to fix me. I don't have to tell you it did not take, not even a little. I hated the hugs, cringed at every I-love-you, shied away from sharing my feelings with the group. But there was this little girl who wouldn't give up on me. And then, fourteen years later and all grown up, she *still* wouldn't give up on me. And this time I wanted every hug, every I love you, wanted to hoard them, stuff them in my pockets, get them tattooed on my arms. But all I knew was being a soldier, that's no kind of life for her, especially not when she had that big, devouring family waiting to take up the slack." He paused and reached out, sliding his finger around the curve of her ear. Even her ears were adorable to him, proving he was the worst sort of besotted fool. "Only it turned out she didn't have that family anymore. She was an orphan, like me. And I realized there was no way I could let her go if it meant she would be on her own. Because, see, she'd been taking care of me since I was twelve, protecting my heart, trying to make it whole. I figure it was about time I returned the favor."

She regarded him in unnatural silence, eyes shiny and big with unshed tears.

"Nothing to say?" he prodded, poking her shoulder. "Two weeks ago I couldn't shut you up."

"I have something to say all right," she snapped, scowling, tears dissolving in a mist of outrage.

"Let's hear it," he prompted, bracing himself for her outburst.

She grasped his shirt with both hands and hauled him closer, until they were nose to nose. "Cutting it a mite close, weren't you, Major?"

He grinned, cupping her face in both his hands. "You're a difficult woman to track, Juniper. I had to call in multiple favors to the intelligence community, some I might never be able to repay. The President sends his best, by the way."

Her lashes fluttered again. "Are you joking?"

He eased closer, lips brushing hers. "Classified."

"Doesn't matter, I don't care anymore." She drew in a shuddery little breath and erased the distance between them, crawling into his lap. "What does a high and mighty major do with his prisoners?"

"I don't know because I'm not a major anymore," he said. His fingers were skimming her neck. He'd like to think that was the cause in the three-second delay before she reacted.

Her body jolted. "What? What did you say?"

"I resigned my commission."

She sat up away from him. "WHAT? Why would you do a fool thing like that?"

"For you. To prove to you I was serious and meant this thing were about to undertake."

"I never wanted that, ever. Bear, you *love* the army. The army is your life."

"Juni." He gripped her waist and tugged her impossibly closer. "I love you. *You* are my life now."

Her eyes softened and she pressed a palm to his cheek. "I appreciate that, more than you could know, but you have to get it back, you have to undo this. Let's go make some calls." She started to slide off his lap, but he anchored her in place.

"That won't exactly be necessary," he said.

"Why? Do you have a new job lined up?" she asked.

"In a manner of speaking. The army was…not inclined to accept my resignation. They offered me a new position." He pressed his lips to her neck.

"What k-kind of position?" she asked, taking a shaky little breath that set his heart thrumming. Her hands gripped his shirt, and he congratulated himself that she seemed to need the support.

"An intelligence job, working under cover, pretending to be a diplomat, heading up a new intelligence sector."

"Diplomat where?" She tipped her head and closed her eyes,

allowing him easier access to her neck. Why had he ever thought for one minute he didn't want this, didn't want her? Now that he had such ready access to her, he could never be without it again, never be without *her* again.

"How would you feel about Africa?"

Her head snapped up. "You know exactly how I feel about Africa."

He grinned. "Yes, in fact I do, which is why I requested it. They gave me my pick of locales, along with a promotion to Lieutenant Colonel."

"Oh, Bear," she murmured, eyes filling with tears again. "Am I going to get to come with you?"

"I wouldn't have it any other way. Of course we'll have to get married. Army regulations."

She sat up. "Now? Today? Because, I mean, I do have the dress. It seems more economical to get double use from it."

He rolled his eyes. "You couldn't wait two seconds for me to ask? Girl, ya vex me. Hold your horses." He leaned around her, opened the glove compartment, and pulled out a small box. "I'm not good with the flowery language, so I'm going to skip all that and tell you we're getting married. And you're going to give me those babies you promised. Four of them."

She gasped, covering her midsection protectively. "Four? That's too many. Two."

He shook his head. "No deal. Two's too few. Three?"

She pretended to think it over. "I could manage three."

"I doubt that. I have great confidence any children you and I produce will be wholly unmanageable. Also I demand boys."

"I don't think I can control that," she said.

"No girls," he warned, going stern again. "I can't handle that much crazy making in multiples."

She circled his neck with her arms. "I'll try. No promises. Now kiss me."

"Blast it, woman, can you let a man be a man and make the first move?"

"You've had twenty years to make the first move. Kiss me or I'll bite you," she said.

"I'm only giving in this once. Don't get used to it," he warned.

"No promises," she repeated.

"Try again, Juniper. I want all the promises, every last one."

"Which promises specifically?" she asked, suspicious now.

"Love, honor, cherish."

"Not obey?" she asked.

"It's my first time being in love, not my first day on planet earth. Of course not obey," he said.

"Not to be difficult here, Bear."

He made a choking sound of repressed incredulity.

"But we're engaged, on our way to be married, and you *still* haven't kissed me. It's beginning to feel very Victorian all up in this car."

"Juniper," he said, shaking his head in exasperation.

"Is it that you don't know how?"

"Juniper," he said, tone changing to annoyance. "You did not just ask me that. Do you honestly think I've never kissed a woman before?"

"You're the one who said you avoided women," she pointed out, matching his annoyed tone with one of her own.

"I said I avoided relationships; I never said I was a monk."

She narrowed her eyes, inspecting him anew. "How not a monk are you, Major Caruthers?"

"That's Lieutenant Colonel now, if you please," he said, amused by her possessive jealousy. He pressed his lips to one side of her neck, "And if you would give me." He pressed his lips to the other side of her neck. "Five minutes of peace." He cupped her face in his hands. "I would show you exactly how un-monastic my existence is about to be." He brushed his lips on hers, feather soft, then pulled back to assess the damage. Her eyes were drowsy and heavy lidded, lips parted, cheeks flushed. "You look like you've been hitting the poppies a little too hard."

"That's it, I'll poppy you," she said and, threading her fingers through his hair, kissed him. And when it was over he had no memory of who made the first move, nor any desire to keep track of who made the next.

They might have remained in the car all day, kissing like love-drunk teenagers, if not for the fact that Juniper slid her hands under his shirt and felt the incision from his surgery. And when he told her he'd been shot the entire time they were together in the jungle, she was so incensed he took her to the chapel to save himself from her wrath.

Then, despite her protests, he carried her over the threshold of their hotel and deposited her gently on the bed.

"I'm still mad at you," she told him. "For lots of reasons, *all* the reasons."

"I'll take it," he replied.

"You're supposed to be terrified, not smile gleefully," she said.

"Can't help it. You're cute when you're mad. Plus you're latched on to me, not very ragey." He tapped her arms, now laced tightly around his neck.

"I can be mad at you and never want to let you go at the same time."

"That's what I'm counting on for the rest of our lives," he said.

"I'm never going to be bored again, am I?" she asked.

"I think we can safely rule it out as a possibility." He lay down beside her with a sigh of contentment, feeling happier and fuller than he thought possible. He was tired, but his eyes didn't want to close, didn't want to stop looking at her, drinking her in. He wondered if she felt the same because her eyes were fastened on his, roaming his face as if trying to memorize it.

"Bear."

"Mm."

"What would you have done if you'd arrived too late, if I'd married Gabe?"

"Would never have happened," he said.

"Are you so certain of your impeccable timing?" she asked.

"No, I'm so certain of your inability to marry him. I saw your face, Juni. You were getting ready to object."

"Don't be smug."

"Can't help it. I got the girl." He tipped forward to kiss her.

"I feel pretty bad about it," she said when the kiss was over.

"Don't. It never would have worked with him. Want to know why?"

"Why?" she asked.

"Because you and me were meant to be. You are and have always been and will always be my girl." His finger reached out and began to lightly trace her face.

"Big talk from a man who doesn't believe in destiny."

"I changed my mind. Rather, you changed my mind. You are my miracle, Juniper. From day one you took this broken, ruined boy and began to put him back together, one persistent, affectionate gesture at a time. And I reckon you'll keep piecing me back together because I keep finding new ways to be broken."

"I guess there's only one thing to do about it," she said.

"What's that?" he asked, smiling preemptively at whatever her words would be.

"Better make it official real quick."

"Oh, I'll make it official," he said, easing closer. "But it definitely won't be quick."

"Have mercy," she murmured.

"No promises," he said and kissed her.

*

*S*ome time later in the night he woke in a sweaty panic. He sat up, gasping for breath. Being a soldier was easier in the day than in the night. There were moments when he slept where he saw faces, heard sounds, sometimes even smelled smells that brought back things he'd rather forget. He hunched into a ball, pressing his forehead to his knees, eyes squeezed tightly shut to try and block the memories.

"John." He jumped when Juniper said his name and laid her little hand on his back.

"I'm fine," he lied. "Go back to sleep."

She ignored him, as usual, and sat up, easing closer to snuggle against him. That snuggle did something to him, something good. His next breath came easier. He opened his eyes and made himself see her and nothing else, and what a sight she was—hair tousled, lips puffy, silken nighty askew. And then she poked him. "You owe me recompense."

"For what, exactly?" He lay down. She snuggled into his embrace, head on his heart that still thrummed with unremembered dread.

"Waking me. And other things. All the things. I keep long accounts and am completely unforgiving."

"And how am I to ever pay this debt?"

"Incrementally, in installments," she said, easing up to kiss him. He kissed her in return, and then it circled back around, the panic. He froze and sucked a shaky breath, pressing his forehead to hers.

"What if I can't actually do this, Juni?"

Instead of answering, she pressed him into the bed and rested her chin on his chest again, this time peering into his face. "Let me to tell you a story." When he didn't reply, she continued, now reaching forward to trace her finger gently around his face. The action was so soothing he closed his eyes, breathing deeply once again. "It's years from now, after you've spied on everyone in Africa. We come back to the states with our three beautiful boys who are all amazing and well-educated, like their daddy."

"And their mama," he interjected. He couldn't see her smile, but he could feel it.

"They can ride a horse, tie a rope, shoot a gun, quote Shakespeare, and cook."

He quirked a brow at that.

"Don't be misogynistic. Boys can cook," she said, poking him.

"Fine, they'll cook," he agreed, sighing as her finger continued its perusal of his features. "They'll still be hooligans."

"Well-educated and proper hooligans," she added, then smoothed her miffed tone and continued. "Anyway, once we return, you'll start spying on people in the states. Maybe you'll work in Washington."

"Perish the thought," he interjected, pressing his lips together when she poked him again.

"And then the best thing happens," she said.

"What?" He could almost picture it, their future, with him happily married and a father. They could have a good life, an amazing life. He saw shadows of it all around as she talked.

"They have babies," she whispered.

He opened his eyes and looked at her. "More babies?"

"Better than babies. *Grand*babies. You'll be a Grampy."

"Huh." He hadn't pictured that far in the future. In truth he had never allowed himself to picture beyond the next dangerous assignment. "Maybe I'll be retired by then."

"You will never retire, it would kill you," she said. "No, someday you'll be on all fours in your office, toting a grandbaby on your back, and the President will enter unannounced. You'll try to pretend it's undignified, but secretly you won't care."

He could picture that, too. It wasn't so far fetched; he'd met three presidents already. "Huh." His gaze landed on Juniper again and he reached for one of her curls, pushing it out of her eyes. "Juni."

"What?"

"Maybe we could have a girl." He could picture a girl like her, with those curls and that dimple and that irrepressible spirit, and it made his heart melt, more than a little. "Just one, though, because not even I am intrepid enough to handle more than that."

"I'll consider it, but, Bear."

"Yes?"

She eased closer, now planting herself provocatively in front of his lips. "It takes two to tango, or so the saying goes."

"My dance teacher told me I was aces at the tango," he said, his breath now stilted and shallow for reasons that had nothing to do with a panic attack.

"Prove it," she whispered.

"Never let it be said that I resisted a challenge," he whispered and kissed her.

Later, when he woke again, calmly this time, he found Juniper cuddled in his embrace, nestled against him, her hair spilling over his arm. He lay still a few moments, staring at her with this sudden realization that nothing that came before mattered, not in any way. Not his career, not his heartache, not his knowledge or training. Only this. And from this moment on his real life began, and every moment after would be the one that counted. For her, for all that they would have together, he would make it count.

With that decided, and his heart and mind clear, he kissed the top of her head and fell asleep, deeply and restfully this time. And every night he was with her, he would continue to sleep the same—secure and at peace, regardless of his career or world events, or anything else. As long as he had Juniper by his side, his life felt whole and unbroken, and so did his heart.

Thank you for reading *The Woman and The Warrior*, book nine in the *Spies Like Us* series. For more books, please check out my website at www.vanessagraybartal.com

ABOUT THE AUTHOR

Vanessa Gray Bartal is a foodie who spends her time trolling bakeries and dreaming of new ways to use sourdough. When she is not baking (or eating), she loves to make music and spend time with her husband, three children, and sheepadoodle in rural Ohio. Her dream is to fill her books with enough coziness and warmth to brighten someone's day and make them smile. She would love to hear from you on Facebook or through email.

9 781953 339416